"Either you want me...or you don't."

"But I think it's always best to sort through these things—" Claudia started to argue.

"I'm really not interested in a conversation right now. Not when all I really want to do is tear off all our clothes."

Her gaze flitted down to his mouth, then back up to meet his eyes again. She drew a ragged breath and her lips parted. It was enough for him, enough to take the chance that she wanted exactly what he did. Slipping his hand behind her neck, he pulled her closer and kissed her.

Her surrender was almost immediate, and Claudia wrapped her arms around his neck and pulled him down beside her until her body was stretched out beneath his.

His desire quickly burned out of control. He needed to touch Claudia, to feel her body beneath his hands.

To kiss her until neither one of them could stop themselves...

Blaze

Dear Reader,

When it came time to find a setting for my newest Quinn trilogy, I was looking for somewhere just a little exotic. And I've always been fascinated by New Zealand. All those incredible landscapes in the *Lord of the Rings* movies. It was the perfect place for my Quinns to live. Of course, now that I've been "traveling" to New Zealand in my literary life, I would love to visit in my real life.

That's one of the things I love most about writing the Quinn saga. There are Quinns all over the world. Where will I find them next? I hope you enjoy this new trilogy and continue to follow the Quinns.

Happy reading,

Kate Hoffmann

The Mighty Quinns: Rogan

Kate Hoffmann

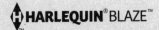

Recycling programs
for this product may
not exist in your area.

ISBN-13: 978-0-373-79814-8

THE MIGHTY QUINNS: ROGAN

Copyright © 2014 by Peggy A. Hoffmann

Printed in U.S.A.

ABOUT THE AUTHOR

Kate Hoffmann began writing for Harlequin in 1993. Since then, she's published nearly eighty books, primarily in the Harlequin Temptation and Harlequin Blaze lines. When she isn't writing, she enjoys music, theater and musical theater. She is active working with high school students in the performing arts. She lives in southeastern Wisconsin with her cat, Chloe.

Books by Kate Hoffmann

Prologue

ROGAN QUINN PEERED out the front window of his grandparents' house, observing the small crowd gathered just outside the garden fence.

"What do you think they want?" he asked.

His twin brother, Ryan, shrugged. "Maybe they want a picture of us crying over Dad, so they can show everyone that we're sad."

"I'm not going to do that for them," Rogan said stubbornly. "I wish they'd just go away and leave us be." He wandered away from the window, his gaze coming to rest on the closed bedroom door. His mother hadn't come out all morning.

She'd had good days and bad in the month since their father's death. On the good days, she managed to appear at the dinner table, usually wrapped in her dressing gown. Food didn't interest her, nor did conversation. She'd just sit, ignoring her four children, before shuffling back to the bedroom.

She'd become a ghost of herself, frail and silent,

her vacant eyes fixed on some imaginary figure in the room.

Rogan had experienced the loss of his father and it had been devastating, but he'd survived the pain. Why had his mother become a victim? Rogan had realized then what love and loss had done to his mother, how it had turned into a poison that sapped her strength and stole her happiness.

Rogan had thought about this so many times over the past few weeks. What was it about the love that existed between his father and mother that was so special? Perhaps it was something only adults understood. Maybe it had to do with sex.

At eight years old, he wasn't sure of all the details of what went on between a man and a woman, but he'd heard stories. The whispered speculation of his friends sprinkled with a bit of firsthand knowledge. He'd even glimpsed a few photos on the internet, though they'd only created more questions than answers.

But Rogan sensed that when he got older, he'd understand his mother's grief. He just never wanted it to happen to him.

Rogan rapped on the bedroom door. "Mum? Can I bring you some tea?"

He waited, hoping that this time she'd reply, but there was only silence. He spun around and strode to the window again, cursing beneath his breath at the media vultures that seemed to hover over them. If they'd just go away, maybe she'd come back, maybe she'd be the mother they'd always known—the mother who laughed with them and loved them.

"I'm going out there," Rogan muttered.

"No, don't," Ryan said, grabbing his arm. "Grandmum said we just have to pretend that they're not there. She'll be home soon. She'll run them off."

"I'm not going to wait for her," Rogan said. "We can do this. Are you coming?"

There was very little that the twins didn't do together, Rogan usually leading and Ryan backing him up. This time, Ryan thought about the request for a long moment, then nodded solemnly. "All right."

Rogan reached for the door and pulled it open. The instant the reporters saw them, they rushed the fence, shouting out questions. Cameras flashed and Rogan held up his hand to ward off the assault. But as he watched them warily, his anger began to build.

With a silent curse, Rogan ran down the front steps and grabbed a clod of dirt from his grandmother's flower bed. With all his strength, he heaved it at the group. "Leave us alone," he cried. "Just go away. We don't want to talk to you."

The shower of dirt was enough to send them all running. Ryan joined him, heaving clumps of soil over the fence until everyone had retreated to their cars. Rogan found a small rock and hit the windscreen of the closest car. As it drove off, he picked up another and heaved it.

One by one, the reporters and photographers scurried away, and when the street in front of their grandparents' home was finally empty, Rogan looked at his brother and smiled. "Cowards," he muttered.

Ryan chuckled. "We really showed them, didn't we."

"You ain't wrong," Rogan replied.

When they returned to the house, Rogan was surprised to find their mother standing at the window, her fingers clutching at the curtains. She gazed at him and Ryan and gave them a weak smile. "Good work," she murmured before moving away.

"Mum? Can I make you a cup of tea?" Rogan asked again.

She stopped and drew a deep breath, and Rogan watched her narrow shoulders rise and fall. "That would be lovely," she said, nodding her head. "I could use a cup of tea."

Rogan and Ryan hurried over to her, each of them taking a hand and leading her to the sofa. They sat down on either side of her and she wrapped her arms around their shoulders and pulled them close, kissing the tops of their heads.

"You're my brave, strong boys," she whispered. "Promise you'll never leave me."

"I promise, Mum," Rogan said.

"Me, too."

Rogan silently made another promise to himself. If this was what love did to his mother, then he wanted no part of it. It only brought despair and loneliness. No girl would ever be worth all that.

_1_

THE SOUND OF his mobile woke Rogan out of a deep sleep. He moaned as he rolled over and searched for the phone on the bedside table.

Delicate feminine fingers smoothed over his belly and he smiled as her warm naked body curled closer.

"Are you going to answer that?" Kaylee murmured.

He squinted his eyes to read the display. If it wasn't his mum or one of his siblings, he could let the call go to voice mail. But when he saw the name of his next expedition client, Dr. Claudia Mathison, Rogan changed his mind. "This will just take a second," he said.

Kaylee sighed. "Make it quick. I have to leave soon."

He sat up and swung his legs over the edge of the bed, then held the phone up to his ear. "Dr. Mathison," he said in a sleep-tinged voice.

"Good morning, Mr. Quinn. I hope I've caught you at a convenient time?" She didn't wait for an answer. "I just have a few more things that I'd like to discuss. Details that are important to make this trip go as smoothly as possible."

Psychologist Claudia Mathison had been calling him at least twice a day over the past few weeks with her little "details," and frankly she was beginning to drive him mad with all her requests. Yes, he understood that this trip would be a big challenge for her five phobic clients. But these were people who lived in the real world, not some invalids who could barely care for themselves.

When Rogan had booked the expedition, he'd bragged to his brothers, Malcolm and Ryan, how this could provide a whole new market for Max Adrenaline, the family's adventure-guiding business. Over the past couple of years, they'd been hit hard by a rival Kiwi—their father's former business partner, in fact—who ran his own outfit off South Island. But Rogan argued that by opening themselves up to new and different clientele, they may just be able to expand on their core business of climbing and trekking expeditions and gain an edge on their competition.

But Rogan also had an ulterior motive for bringing in new business. Though at first, he'd been happy to work with his brothers and carry on the memory of his father, he'd never intended it to be his lifelong profession. Once the business was squarely on its feet, he'd always planned to go his own way. But the business never seemed to operate in the black, and lately he'd begun to wonder if there wasn't more to life than climbing mountains and crossing glaciers.

He wasn't sure what he was looking for, but whatever it was, he was sure it would make him happy again.

He'd grown weary of the constant stress and his current rootless existence. He wanted to see new places, discover new adventures, but he'd been stuck guiding the same itineraries for the past four years.

Adding new routes was always a risk for the company and a huge investment in time and equipment. But if he and his brothers could find an easy source of income, one that didn't involve gambling their capital, then maybe he could finally walk away from Max Adrenaline and live his own life. Which meant he had to keep Claudia Mathison happy.

"What can I do for you this morning, Dr. Mathison?"

"I've been going over the tent pairings and I think we're going to need two extra tents," she said. "In fact, it might just be better if they all had their own tents, if that wouldn't be too much trouble. I'm dealing with very mercurial personalities here, and I want everything to go as smoothly as possible."

"No, it wouldn't be too much trouble to double the number of tents from three to six," he said. "As long as your patients don't mind carrying their own. Just keep in mind our two-person tents for this type of expedition are eight pounds. So everyone will have to carry that extra weight on their packs."

"Eight pounds? That's not much," she said.

"It is when you're climbing a steep trail," he countered. "Which we will be doing on this trip."

"Perhaps you could send someone ahead with the tents?" she suggested.

"Dr. Mathison, I thought you wanted to challenge your clients. Take them out of their comfort zone. I've planned a week of survival training and wilderness camping. If you want Max Adrenaline to do all the work, then we should just make reservations at the nearest spa and settle in with massages and mineral baths."

A long silence fell between them and Rogan bit his lower lip. He knew better than to sound off like that, especially with a new client. But if this was how she meant to go on, the trip was going to be a rough ride for them both. In addition to her ever-growing list of necessities to calm her phobic patients' fears, now she was taking away the basic challenge of the trek. This woman seriously needed to loosen up.

Still, they were desperate for her business. "I'm sorry," he said. "Maybe I should ring you back after I've had my coffee."

"Perhaps that would be best," she said. "I'll speak with you later. Ring me at twelve forty-five my time. That would be three forty-five for you. I have a twenty-minute opening in my schedule and we can work out the final details."

Rogan rubbed his forehead. If it was nine in the morning where he was in Auckland, then it was seven in the morning in Sydney, where she lived. "Do you always get to work this early?" he asked.

"I don't need much sleep," she said. "I'll talk to you later."

"All right. Catch you later."

Rogan flopped back down on the bed and threw his arm over his eyes. A few seconds later, Kaylee pressed a kiss to his chest. He looked down to see her smiling at him, her blond hair tumbled around her face. "Good morning," she said.

"Morning," he replied. "Sorry about that."

"No worries," she replied. "It's time to get up. I've got a lot of packing to do today."

Rogan frowned. "Packing? Are you going on holiday?"

Kaylee gave him an uneasy smile. "No. Actually, I'm relocating."

"Really? Getting a new place?"

"More like a…a new life," she said. She sat up beside him and pulled the bedcovers up around her naked body. "I meant to tell you last night, but then we had a few drinks and things got randy between us. I'm moving down to Christchurch with Denny Fitzgerald. He's gotten a promotion and he asked if I'd come with him. And I said yes."

"Wait," Rogan said, shaking his head. "You and Denny?"

Kaylee shrugged. "Yeah. He's a nice guy, Rogan. We've been getting closer. He's sweet and he loves me and he wants to make a life with me. And he's around."

"When did this happen?"

"It's been going on for about a year, but nothing official. Until now, that is."

"Why haven't I heard about it?"

"I don't know. Maybe because you're never home. Listen, you're a nice bloke, Rogan, but a girl can't live on a few weeks of incredible sex three or four times a year. As good as it all is, it's just not enough. I want something…more. I want a husband and a family. Denny can give that to me."

"I could do more for you," Rogan said. But even as the words came out of his mouth, he realized they weren't true. If he really had wanted more with Kaylee, he would have made it happen. He'd been perfectly content with what they'd had—great sex every two or three months when he happened to be home…and then not a moment spent worrying about her in between.

Kaylee reached out and smoothed her hand over his cheek. "That's just what you think you want," she murmured. "But I know you. You could never be tied down. It's just not you."

"Yeah," Rogan muttered. "But occasionally I wish it was."

A wistful smile curled the corners of her mouth. "Denny and I are going to be very happy."

Rogan reluctantly nodded. "I hope he appreciates what a great girl he's getting."

"I think he does." She crawled over him and began to search the bedroom for her panties. "You'll find someone else. Women are always attracted to men like you. At least for a while."

Rogan watched silently as Kaylee slipped into her clothes. He wanted to pull her back into bed and have his way with her just once more. But that would serve only one purpose—to make him feel worse about her leaving. Of all the girls he'd dated, she'd been his favorite. Though he and Kaylee had never defined their relationship, beyond enjoying each other in the bedroom, he'd still looked forward to seeing her again at the end of every trip. She was sweet and sexy and undemanding—always satisfied with what he had to offer. Until now.

She plopped down on the bed and tugged on her shoes, then turned to him. "So, I guess it's goodbye, then."

"I guess so," Rogan murmured.

She bent over him and brushed a quick kiss on his lips. "It's been fun. And I'll miss you. Take care and don't fall off any mountains."

Rogan reached up and smoothed a strand of flaxen hair out of her eyes. "I'll miss you, too."

She laughed, her eyes sparkling with a devilish glint. "No, you won't. You'll have a new girl in your bed by the end of the week."

Kaylee jumped up and walked to the door, turning back just once to blow him a kiss. "Ta ta, Rogan. Have a nice life."

"Ta ta, Kaylee. Take care."

He listened to her footsteps as they echoed through the cottage, then shut his eyes as the front door closed. "Bloody hell," he muttered.

The sound of the front door opening ended his temporary depression and Rogan grinned. Maybe she'd changed her mind already. Denny Fitzgerald was a tosser, and no sane woman would choose him. "Back so soon?" he shouted.

"It's me."

A few moments later, Rogan's older brother, Mal, walked through the bedroom door. "I met Kaylee on the way out. Rotten news, that."

Rogan cursed softly, then crawled out of bed and

grabbed his jeans, tugging them on as he walked to the loo. "When did you find out about her and Denny Fitzgerald?"

"Dana told me a few months ago. I assumed you knew." Dana, their sister, usually wasn't great about keeping a secret.

"Just found out this morning," Rogan said as he began to brush his teeth. "Can't say I blame her. I can't offer her much of a life." He looked out the bathroom door. "What are you doing here?"

Mal held up a large envelope. "I brought you this. It's the first three chapters of the biography Amy is writing about Dad. I thought you might like to read it. It's quite good, if I can say so about my own girlfriend's writing."

Rogan grabbed a towel and wiped his mouth, then wandered back out to the living room. When he didn't grab the envelope right away, Mal shrugged and dropped it on the table in front of the sofa.

Rogan wasn't sure how he felt about everything that was happening in regards to Max Quinn. The book, the expedition to recover his body from Everest and the publicity that was sure to follow. He understood why Mal was so keen on it all, but there was some instinct buried deep inside Rogan that shouted caution.

But then, Rogan knew more about his father than Mal did—than Mal *wanted* to know. He'd first heard the rumors about their father on a trekking expedition to Annapurna. A few blokes from another team were chatting over dinner and the conversation had turned to women climbers, and one in particular. Annalise Montgomery. He hadn't meant to eavesdrop, but when he heard his father's name mentioned, he spun around to face the other climbers. The pair quickly went silent when they recognized him and they'd refused to say more. Rogan wished that had been the end of it.

Rogan sat down on the sofa and regarded the envelope pensively, then reached out to pick it up. "Are you sure you really want to open all this up again, Mal? What if we find out something we don't want to know? Something that hurts Mum?"

"She thinks the book is a good idea," Mal said.

"But she's still wobbling on the expedition. She said as much to me last week," Rogan countered.

"She'll come round. We've almost worked out the funding. And you can't tell me you're not interested in climbing Everest."

Truthfully, Rogan *was* interested in the climb. He wouldn't have clients to worry about and it would be different. Max Adrenaline had never offered an Everest expedition in deference to his mother. Still, he didn't expect that she was going to approve of all three of her sons climbing the peak that had killed her husband.

"I still think we ought to discuss the book," Rogan said. "All of us. You, me, Ryan and Dana."

Mal shrugged. "Getting all four of us together at one time is nearly impossible. And what difference would it make?" He stood up. "Now, I have to find my old bike. Have you seen it? Ryan was using it last winter. Amy wants a bike with a basket so she can run errands around town without the car."

"Haven't a clue. Why don't you just buy her a new bike?"

"I suggested that, but she's on an austerity kick right now. She says we should start saving our money. So we can start a family."

"You're not even married yet," Rogan said, staring at his brother.

"I know. But we're talking about making it official. And after that, who can say. We both want kids, so it might happen sooner rather than later."

"Jaysus, Mal, things are moving a bit fast, don't you think?"

"No," Mal said, shaking his head. "Now that we've decided we want to be together, we're moving forward. Just as Dad always said, 'one foot in front of the other.' That's the only way to get anywhere in life."

"How is that going to affect your schedule?"

"Amy realizes we'll have to be apart for long periods of time. But she says she understands that's the way it has to be. We'll work it out. Although I would like to cut back a bit on leading the long trips. I was hoping to talk to you and Ryan about that."

Rogan ran his fingers through his tousled hair. So much for his own plans to leave the family business behind. Now that Mal was talking about marriage, that would leave only Ryan to guide the big expeditions and he couldn't do it alone. The business and the family would surely suffer.

"Sure," Rogan said. "No problem."

"Great. It'll only be for a while. Business is going to pick up and we'll be able to afford to hire more guides. At some point, I'd like to take just a few trips a year."

Rogan pushed to his feet. Max Adrenaline had always been Mal's baby. He was the one who'd convinced Rogan and Ryan to sign on. And now, he was the one anxious to step back. "So you managed to find the one woman in the entire bleedin' world who was willing to put up with the lifestyle. How did you manage that?"

He brushed past Mal and walked to the kitchen, his frustration slowly simmering. Why were things always so much easier for Mal? It always seemed as though he had complete control over everything—his life, his emotions, his women.

"Don't take your pissy attitude out on me," Mal said as he followed him through the back. "It's not my fault Kaylee decided to run off with Fitzgerald."

Rogan drew a deep breath before he began to make a pot of coffee. "It's not her. I just had a bad start to my day."

In truth, he couldn't remember the last time he'd had a *good* start to his day. Nothing seemed to move him anymore, not even the view from the top of a mountain or the smell of a deep, damp rain forest. There was something missing, but he couldn't put his finger on it.

Had he been free to live his life as he pleased, he'd probably escape to some monastery in Tibet and try to suss it all out. But he had responsibilities he couldn't escape, responsibilities that Mal reminded him of nearly every day.

"Well, chin up," Mal said, repeating another familiar family phrase.

That was how the Quinns had always dealt with problems—chin up, one foot in front of the other, stiff upper lip.

"Right-o," Rogan muttered.

"Besides, your new client can't be as bad as you're making out," Mal said.

"She rang this morning with yet another list of things she wants to discuss. Is there a nit she hasn't picked yet? I'm thinking I ought to pass her off to you. You could handle her nagging better than me."

"She's your client," Mal said. "And what's that supposed to mean? I can handle the nagging?"

Rogan chuckled. "You're the one with a permanent woman in your life."

"Yeah. But Amy doesn't nag me."

"Never?"

Mal shook his head. "No. In fact, we get on quite well. I love being with her. There isn't anyone I'd rather spend my time with."

"Why?" Rogan asked. "What is it about her? Why is she so special?"

Mal sat silently for a long moment as he tried to put his thoughts into words. "She makes me laugh. And I make her laugh. I reckon if we have that then there's not much that's going to tear us apart."

Rogan leaned back into the sofa and closed his eyes. Maybe that was what he was missing—someone who could make him laugh. Someone who would always be there to brighten up his days and nights.

"It's a weeklong trip right here on the North Island," Mal murmured. "You've taught survival skills how many times? It's good money. Just get it done. You'll be home and hosed before you know it."

"Yeah, yeah," Rogan admitted. "How are antibacterial wipes required for survival? And she seems to be unusually obsessed with the amount of toilet tissue I'll be bringing along. You can see why I have my concerns. I get the feeling I'm going to be babysitting a lot of needy children rather than five adults."

"Keep her happy," Mal said. "This is a whole new market for us. Besides, she paid up front and we've spent the money already."

"That's probably why she paid in advance. Just so I couldn't cancel." He sighed. "I'll get through it. Maybe not with my sanity intact, but I'll make it work."

"Good," Mal said. "Now put a shirt on and I'll take you to brekkie. And then we'll go over Dr. Mathison's lists and make sure everything is confirmed."

"Do you think I ought to go after her?" Rogan asked.

"Dr. Mathison?"

"No. Kaylee. Maybe she's the one who can make me laugh and I just haven't sussed that out yet. I'd hate for her to marry that tosser before I was sure of how I really felt about her."

"Believe me," Mal said, "if you loved her, you'd know it. It would hit you like a brick to the head and a kick to the gut. Trust me on this."

Rogan glanced over at his brother. He really had no choice but to trust him. Mal was the only one of his siblings who'd owned up to experiencing that emotion. Though Rogan would understand if Kaylee wasn't the one for him, he couldn't imagine there was anyone better out there. Not that he ever wanted to fall in love like Mal.

For now, he'd focus on his next trip, and making sure

Dr. Claudia Mathison was pleased with the experience. He could worry about the rest of his life later.

CLAUDIA WATCHED AS the baggage carousel began to turn. She bit back a yawn as she observed her five patients, all in various states of distress. They'd finally managed to get on a plane from Sydney to Auckland after three aborted attempts to board. Then the three-hour flight had been a stress-filled nightmare, as every one of the five had had some complaint.

Emma Wilson, her germophobe, had spent the flight washing every surface around her with antibacterial wipes—while wearing a surgical mask. The claustrophobic Millie Zastrow had paced the aisle between her seat and the bathroom like a caged animal. Eddie Findlay, who was agoraphobic, spent the flight muttering to himself from beneath a blanket and scaring away the passengers sitting around him. Leticia Macullum had self-medicated with wine to the point that she fell asleep shortly after takeoff and hadn't even been bothered by the height, usually a crippling fear for her. And Marshall Block had spent his time carefully surveying the floor for any errant pests that might have taken up residence on the plane, as he was an insectophobe.

There were moments, many more of late, that Claudia had to wonder whether she'd picked the right profession. She'd worked with this group for two years and not one of the five had conquered their fear. In fact, they'd just added more fears to the list. Surely she should have helped at least one of her patients by now.

Last year, she'd taken on a part-time teaching job at

a small university in Sydney and was considering a career change. Maybe she'd be better at academia than she was at clinical work. And most of her patients would be fine with other doctors. Maybe they'd even be better off.

She glanced over at the group and felt a surge of guilt. They all seemed to enjoy coming to group therapy, and though they often argued among themselves, they'd grown to be a family of sorts—a dysfunctional family, but a family.

Some days, they seemed so close to resolving their fears, and other days, they became overwhelmed by them. She'd hoped this trip would push them out of their comfort zones. None in the group had ever traveled, chained to their day-to-day routines by their fears. They all preferred a controlled environment with their usual coping mechanisms firmly in place.

So she'd decided that maybe by throwing them into a new situation they'd learn how to exist in the real world—without her help. So far, she'd been wrong.

"All of you stay right here," she said. "I'm just going to run to the ladies'."

"Take these," Emma Wilson said, holding out a packet of wipes. "You don't know what kind of plague is growing on all those fixtures. Ebola, typhus, meningitis. I could make you a list."

"I'm sure that's not necessary," Claudia said. "And I think I'll risk it without the wipes."

She spun on her heel and hurried down the concourse, tears pushing at the corners of her eyes. This was turning into an unmitigated disaster. Everything she'd worked so hard to achieve was now in jeopardy, and all because of this one stupid idea. It had sounded so good on paper, and she'd imagined how she'd put her successful story into a journal article or even a book. She'd even devised a name for it—adventure-based therapy.

Claudia wandered over to an empty row of chairs and sat down. The tears began to tumble down her cheeks and she allowed herself the release, hoping a good cry would restore her emotional balance.

Covering her face with her hands, she let the frustration out along with her tears, scolding herself for her hubris. If she was going to teach, she'd need to publish. But she'd been so anxious to find a new direction for her professional life that she'd risked the well-being of her clients and her reputation. If they could barely make it through a three-hour flight, how would they finish the rest of the week?

"Are you all right?"

Claudia looked up to find a man standing in front of her, his handsome face etched with concern. "Of course I am. Why would you assume I wasn't?"

"You're sitting alone in a nearly deserted airport at midnight and you're crying. It was just a wild guess."

Her cheeks warmed and she wondered if he was trying to pick her up. Nothing about her demeanor would lead him to think that she was open to that. Maybe he had some kind of white-knight complex that compelled him to help people in need. He smiled and a shiver raced down her spine. Or maybe he was just a nice guy showing a bit of concern for a stranger.

"I'm just taking a moment to vent," she explained.

"This whole day has been one disaster after another." She drew a ragged breath. "I just had to release some of the stress." Claudia held her arms out and shook her hands, closing her eyes as she worked the tension out of her muscles. When she opened her eyes again, she found him staring at her.

"Stress can kill you," he said. "Can I get you anything? A cup of tea? Something to eat?"

Oh, gosh, he really was sweet. Either that, or he was some sleazy lothario, cruising airports at midnight, looking for vulnerable women. No, that couldn't be it. He was far too handsome to need to resort to such brazen tactics.

"I'm really quite fine," she said. "A few more moments and then I'll get back to my group."

"Your group?" He chuckled softly. "You wouldn't be Dr. Mathison, would you?"

"I would," she said. "How did you—" Claudia paused. "And you're Rogan Quinn?" She forced a smile. "Of course you are." Fresh tears pushed at the corners of her eyes. "This is just fabulous. I'm supposed to be in control and here you find me blubbering like an idiot."

Rogan shook his head. "You don't look like an idiot. And sometimes we can all use a good blubber," he teased. "To be honest, you've seemed wound a bit tight when we've spoken on the phone."

"What?"

"This trip is supposed to be fun. I see I have my work cut out for me."

"I'm not the one who needs help," she said, sending him a defiant glare.

"Oh, but I'm sure I can do you some good, as well," Rogan replied. "Loosen up. You're on holiday."

"I am quite loose, thank you very much." Claudia wiped the last of her tears from her cheeks. "And I'm not on holiday. This is work for me. No different from my therapy sessions in the office."

"Work or not, I've made reservations at a nearby hotel," he said. "I figured a decent night's rest would be just what the doctor ordered." He held out his hand. "Come on, then. Pull yourself together and we'll move on."

She placed her hand in his. It would have been rude to ignore the kind gesture. And he really was trying to help. But Claudia wasn't prepared for her reaction to his touch. Her heart skipped a beat and for a moment, she forgot to breathe.

It had been such a long time since she'd been with a man, so long in fact that she'd forgotten what desire felt like. But that wasn't what she was feeling here, was it? Yes, he was handsome and sexy and had a smile that could melt anyone's reserve. But they'd just met.

She got to her feet and managed to find the where-withal to speak. "Thank you." She gently pulled her hand from his, but as they walked down the concourse toward the baggage claim, he smoothed his palm across the small of her back.

They weren't in a crowd. There was no need to touch her, yet he seemed quite comfortable doing so. *Stop!* This was crazy, trying to analyze his every behavior and her accompanying reaction. He was simply being polite. But, oh, it felt so delicious to experience this excitement again.

"So, you had a pleasant flight?" he asked.

Claudia laughed out loud. "You're kidding me, right?"

"I was just making conversation."

"Mr. Quinn, I—"

"You can call me Rogan."

No way. Referring to him in such a familiar way would make it even more difficult to keep her thoughts professional. Rogan. It was an unusual name…for an unusual man.

There was something about him that was magnetic. A charisma, a charm that was completely irresistible. When he smiled, she felt as if she were the only woman in the world.

She'd known men like him. They'd always been the ex-boyfriends or ex-husbands of her clients. Men who could make a woman fall in love so hard that she lost all ability to make rational decisions. Rogan Quinn was a dangerous sort.

"Perhaps you should go on ahead and arrange transportation to the hotel," she suggested, hoping for a moment alone.

"I have our van waiting in the car park. Everything is taken care of."

Claudia felt all of her tension slowly dissipate. She fought the urge to throw her arms around his neck and kiss him. Though she wasn't usually prone to displays of public affection, this man was competent and organized and quite pleasant. He might be a flirt, but he'd just rescued her from disaster. He deserved some type of compensation.

"This will definitely be reflected in your tip," she murmured.

As soon as she said it, Claudia regretted the back-handed compliment. It made him sound so mercenary, when he'd only been trying to please her with his professionalism.

"It's all part of the job," Rogan replied.

She gave him a quick glance, trying to read his expression. He didn't appear to be insulted. Claudia prided herself on her ability to anticipate problems and deal with them before they turned into disasters. To him, she must look like an incompetent boob. "I hope this delay won't cause too many problems with the itinerary."

"I think, from now on, we need to keep the itinerary as flexible as possible."

"But everything is planned. I want to make efficient use of our—"

He reached out and pressed a finger to her lips. "Loose. Easy. Go with the flow. I've got it all covered. Trust me."

Claudia nodded silently. She wasn't known for her flexibility. Every last minute of her day, her week, her life, was planned. She didn't do anything unless it appeared in her date book. But she wasn't beyond experiencing something new, moving out of her own comfort zone. Maybe this trip could be a learning experience for her as well as her clients.

They walked together to the baggage claim carousel and found her patients huddled in a group, deep in discussion. When they saw Claudia, they quickly pulled apart, shooting her nervous looks. Emma stepped forward, squaring her shoulders as she prepared to speak. "We're tired and we're hungry," she said. She glanced around at her compatriots and then all nodded their agreement. "We want to go to a hotel and we want separate rooms."

"And room service," Eddie Findlay, Claudia's agoraphobe, whispered. "I'm not eating in a public restaurant."

"I'll need a ground-floor room," Leticia Macullum added. "If there's a fire, I won't be jumping from any windows.

"No lifts me for me," Millie Zastrow added. "And I have to have a large room. With big windows. That open."

"But, Millie, I thought we'd conquered your fear of lifts," Claudia said. "Remember our coping mechanism? The counting game?"

"No lifts," Millie insisted, crossing her arms in front of her.

"I'm sure we can accommodate all your requests," Rogan said in a genial tone. "Let's gather up your luggage. I'll just go fetch the van and we'll be off."

Emma smiled in triumph. "Good. We're all very exhausted from the trip."

"Do you know how long it's been since the establishment was fumigated? I—I have a problem with insects."

Rogan turned to Marshall Block. "I'm not sure. But I'll ask when we arrive."

Claudia stood back and watched as Rogan got them

all moving toward the exit. She knew he was an experienced guide. That was why she'd requested him. But she hadn't expected him to be so patient and understanding. He seemed to sense the mood of the group and adjust his tone accordingly. Surprisingly, the entire group fell into line behind him.

Rogan only had to address a few of their concerns about the service record of his van before he managed to get everyone safely inside. As they drove to the hotel, Claudia studied his profile in the darkened interior. His rugged good looks would cause any red-blooded woman's gaze to linger a bit longer.

His dark hair was shaggy and thick and she decided the only grooming he gave it was a quick comb-through with his fingers. His deep tan set off perfect teeth and eyes that were as blue as the sky on a clear day. Though she preferred a smooth-shaven man, the stubble did give him a rugged appearance. But it was his smile, so warm and engaging, that she found so attractive.

She let her gaze drift lower and made a careful catalog of his other physical attributes. He was tall and lanky, but she suspected that beneath the casual clothes, he had a beautiful body. Not soft and pale, like most of the academics she'd dated, but hard and muscled, like a man who spent most of his time in harsh conditions.

No one spoke on the way to the hotel, and the ride was mercifully short. When they got out of the van, Rogan helped carry the baggage inside, then gathered them all at the reception desk. "Let's meet here at noon tomorrow. I'll leave you all to get brekkie on your own.

Just put it on your room tab and it will be covered for you."

"What are we going to do tomorrow?" Leticia asked in a timid voice.

"I haven't quite worked that out yet," he said. "But it won't involve any airplane flights."

That seemed to bring a chorus of relieved sighs. Claudia cleared her throat and said to her patients, "Why don't we plan on getting together for a group session tomorrow morning at eleven? We should discuss what happened today and—"

"I think it would be better if we left today in the past and started fresh in the morning," Rogan interrupted. "No use dwelling on it. It's important to keep moving forward."

Claudia bit back a gasp. It was terribly presumptuous of him to countermand her authority at such an early point in the trip. But it would be unprofessional to make an issue out of it in front of the others. "Perhaps that would be best," she said.

She didn't want to start an argument now; she'd take Rogan aside later and quietly inform him of his error.

Her mind flashed an image of the two of them alone, but it wasn't a congenial meeting of minds that she imagined. To her shock, the scene was intimate, the lights dimmed, the mood relaxed. Claudia shook herself out of the brief fantasy and looked over at Rogan, only to find him staring at her.

"Yes, we'll meet in the lobby at noon," she said. Her clients all nodded in agreement, then lined up to check in to their rooms. "I'll leave you to take care of the details," she said to Rogan.

She grabbed her bag and headed toward the comfortable sofas, but at the last moment she made a detour toward the hotel bar. Though she'd never been much of a drinker, right now she needed something to bolster her spirits. This trip would be the biggest challenge of her career. But it could also be her greatest success. It could open doors and position her as a new voice with a fresh approach. She could imagine any number of universities interested in her groundbreaking work—maybe even a few outside Australia.

And yet, here she was, ready to give it all up and get on a plane back to Sydney, with or without her group. If she really wanted this to work, she'd have to gather her resolve and fight through the frustrations. Besides, she couldn't help but be a bit curious as to what Rogan Quinn might have planned for them all. Even if she didn't have much confidence in her plan right now, he seemed to think it would work.

"Trust the expert," she murmured to herself. After all, she'd put her career in his hands.

He found her sitting in the bar at the hotel, nursing a martini with two olives. Rogan hadn't paid much attention when Claudia had wandered off. But once he'd gotten all her patients checked in to their rooms, carried Leticia's luggage up the stairs to her second-floor room and devised an escape route for her in case of fire, he'd realized that Claudia hadn't yet checked in.

Rogan sat down on the stool beside her. "Whiskey," he murmured to the bartender. "Neat."

Claudia glanced over at him, her eyes bleary. It looked as if she'd been "venting" again, but her cheeks weren't damp and her nose wasn't red. Even now, completely exhausted and most likely drunk, she was beautiful—and probably completely unaware of it.

Her dark hair, constrained earlier by a neat clip, now fell in waves around her face, and her lipstick was smudged. She wore a tailored blazer and a white blouse that now seemed a bit wilted.

"Shouldn't you be in bed?" she asked, reaching for her nearly empty glass.

"I was going to ask you the same thing. You look like hell."

She held up her glass in a mock toast, then drained the tiny bit of vodka in the bottom. Then she popped the two olives into her mouth and considered his statement. "Great. Then I feel as good as I look." Frowning, she held out her glass to the bartender and he dutifully prepared another and slid it across the bar.

"How many of those have you had?"

"How many of these have I had?" Claudia asked the bartender.

The young man held up three fingers.

"Including that one?" Rogan asked.

He nodded.

"I think she's had enough," Rogan ordered.

"You're the man in charge," she murmured, pointing at him.

"They're all safely into their rooms," he continued. "I don't think you'll have any problems until morning."

"Thank you," she said, taking a sip of her new drink. "It's been a very enlightening day. I've come face-to-face with my limitations as a therapist and I feel a bit bruised right now." She giggled. "And just a little drunk."

"I know I told you to loosen up, but I didn't mean for you to get pissed at the first available opportunity."

"Just following orders." She turned to smile at him. "I am most definitely loose."

This was unexpected, Rogan mused. When he'd challenged her to relax, he hadn't expected her to go so far. But now that she had, he'd make sure she got back to her room with her dignity intact.

"So, tell me about yourself, Mr. Quinn." She leaned closer and bumped against his shoulder. "What makes you tick?"

"Are you trying to analyze me?" Rogan asked.

"Oh, I don't have the energy for that tonight. I'm just making polite conversation."

"What would you like to know?"

"Are you married?"

"No," he said. She got right to the point. But he wasn't sure what her point was. Did his relationship status make a difference to her?

"Explain," she ordered.

He gave her a dubious look. "Explain? I'm not sure what you mean."

"Exactly how does a man as attractive as you are,

with a voice like yours…" She took a deep breath and closed her eyes. "And who smells as great as you do. How is it that you aren't happily married with three children and a dog?"

"I guess I haven't found the right woman yet."

"You are interested in women, aren't you? You can tell me." She pressed a finger to her lips. "I'm a professional."

"Yes," he said, nodding. "I'm interested in women."

Claudia sighed, then took another sip of her drink. "Oh, good. It would be such a shame if you weren't. She drew a deep breath. "So, do you have a girlfriend?"

"Do you always interrogate strangers like this?" he asked. "Or is this the martini talking?"

"I always do this," she said. "I have a natural curiosity. Most people don't mind. In fact, most people enjoy talking about their problems, and when they find out I'm a psychologist, they're happy to get a free session."

"Well, I don't require your services, Dr. Mathison."

"Everyone has at least a few problems worth talking about," she countered.

"Like your need to control every single moment of this trip? That's going to be a problem. Maybe we should talk about that."

She considered his statement for a long moment, then nodded. "Point taken. I have my own little demons. But I'm curious about yours."

"I don't have any." Rogan recognized the lie. But the last person he wanted peering into the dark corners of his mind was Dr. Claudia Mathison.

"I'll make you a deal," she said.

"What's that?"

"If you get me to loosen up, then I get to peek inside your head."

"You want to x-ray my brain?"

"No," she said with a giggle. "I want to shrink your head. I want to figure you out. If you manage to loosen me up, then I get to analyze you. You have to answer all my questions."

"Believe me, you won't find anything of interest inside my head. I'm a pretty normal bloke."

"There's no such thing. Besides, look at yourself. You're gorgeous—and you're not married. Not even attached."

"How do you know I'm not attached?"

"Because if you were, you wouldn't be staring at me like you want to kiss me," she said.

Rogan gasped. "I do not—"

"Oh, come now. You're most definitely flirting with me. You touch me every opportunity you get." She nodded at his hand resting on her leg, his fingers in hers. "See there? So tell me all your secrets."

Rogan downed his whiskey, then motioned for another. He'd never met a woman like Claudia, a woman who said exactly what was on her mind the moment it occurred to her. He was used to expending all his energy trying to figure out the opposite sex. Women never said exactly what they meant, they were always playing some sort of game.

Maybe that was why he'd been reluctant to make a romantic commitment. How could a guy trust his heart to a woman when he couldn't be sure when she was telling the truth and when she was lying? "I don't have any secrets," Rogan said. "Maybe we should talk about tomorrow's itinerary."

"Classic avoidance," she said.

"I'm doing my job," he countered.

"I'm sure everything will go exactly as planned."

"You can't plan for every eventuality, Dr. Mathison. I—"

"You should call me Claudia," she interrupted. "Unless you deliberately want to maintain a distance between us. Which doesn't seem to be the case since you're still touching me."

Rogan looked down to find his fingers still tangled in hers. Hell, he hadn't even realized what he was doing. He gently pulled his hand away.

"I might change our plan a bit," he said. "I don't want to stress the group out too much on the first day."

"It was a certified disaster today, wasn't it?" she muttered. "I should have planned better. But it was just like a— What do you call that when snow slides down the side of a hill and—"

"Avalanche?"

"Yes! An avalanche. It started small and it just got bigger and bigger until I couldn't seem to stop it. Avalanche. Why couldn't I remember that word?"

"You're exhausted. Your brain isn't functioning at full capacity. And you're working on your third martini."

"I require very little sleep," she informed him.

Jaysus, she was a quirky little thing, Rogan mused,

suppressing a smile. "Yes, you mentioned that on the phone."

"I know I can be a pain in the arse," Claudia said. "And I'm sorry if I was overly demanding. I could tell you were irritated, but it always pays to be prepared. I like to be prepared. You can appreciate that, can't you?"

"I can," Rogan agreed. "But then, there is something to be said for spontaneity. Interesting things happen when you don't plan for them."

"I suppose so," Claudia said. "I didn't expect you to be so attractive. I didn't plan on that."

He chuckled softly. "What did you expect?"

"Someone older. Rougher around the edges. More commanding."

"I'm not commanding?" Rogan asked.

"No. I mean, you're obviously very competent. But I'd call you affable. Yes, that's it. You're affable."

Was that really her first impression? Rogan wondered. Women were usually much more taken by his charm and devastating good looks. Or so they said. "And you're drunk," he said.

"Maybe," Claudia admitted. "Just a little. But you'll still be affable in the morning."

For some reason, the sentiment seemed to amuse her and she got caught up in a long fit of giggles. Rogan found her loss of control just as endearing as her joke and he joined her until they were both giddy and breathless. Claudia took a deep breath. "I feel better now," she said.

"Better than having a good cry?" he asked.

"Much better."

"Come on then," he said. "I've got you a room. You can finish your drink there. That way, if you pass out, you'll already be in bed."

He picked up her glass and waited while she got to her feet. Her bag was still sitting next to the stool. "Can you have someone bring her bag up to room 1114?" he asked the bartender.

"I can get my own bag," Claudia protested. "I'm not that drunk." She bent down to pick it up but had to reach out to balance herself on the back of the stool. "Then again, maybe I am."

"Come on, Doc. Just put one foot in front of the other. The lift isn't that far."

"You are a very good guide," Claudia said, waving her finger at him.

It took a bit of time for her to balance her purse and her bag, but then she took off at an amazingly brisk pace, her shoes clicking smartly against the marble floor as he followed. When they got to the lift, she pushed the button and stared at the lights above the door. He stood behind her, wondering what was going through her head.

Rogan knew exactly was going through *his* mind. His gazed drifted down to her bum and he contemplated the curves beneath the unfaded denim jeans. By appearances, she seemed to be the model of perfection, right down to her painted fingernails. But he got the sense that the prim and proper exterior was hiding a mess of contradictions on the inside.

He'd always heard that about shrinks, that they were usually more crazy than their patients. She'd been crazy enough to try to get five of her phobic patients on a plane together and fly them all to New Zealand, and crazy enough to plan this trip.

But though it was probably going to be a hellish week for him, he relished the chance to get to know her a little better.

Rogan had always been attracted to "easy" girls. Those who didn't fuss over their appearance and who were ready to surf or bike or hike at a moment's notice. That was obviously not Claudia Mathison. She was a planner, the kind of woman he usually found irritating. And yet, he found himself strangely attracted to her. Or maybe it wasn't attraction, but curiosity.

Still, he'd be wise to temper the attraction with a healthy dose of suspicion. She wanted to analyze him, and he wasn't about to bare his soul to a stranger, even if she was a beautiful, sexy, intriguing woman.

Revealing his insecurities and vulnerabilities wouldn't do either one of them any good. She'd see him as flawed and he'd be constantly on edge, waiting for her to use the information against him. Hell, he hadn't even revealed his innermost fears to his own brothers, and they were the two people he trusted most in the world.

Then again, maybe that was why he'd never fallen in love. He'd never trusted a woman enough to let her get close…really close. That kind of trust was a double-edged sword. It could open up a person to love but it could also destroy him in a single blow. Look what had happened to his mother. No, he'd keep his heart to himself.

But her challenge did intrigue him. He was sure he

could get the good doctor to loosen up—without revealing any of his secrets.

The lift doors opened and she stumbled inside. Rogan followed her and they stood together as the door closed. She was closest to the control panel and he waited for her to push the button for the eleventh floor.

He smiled to himself. She'd fixed her gaze on the lights above the door again, her pretty face crunched into a frown. "This lift is broken," she finally said. "It's not moving. Or is it moving?" She leaned back against the wall. "Maybe I'm the one that's moving."

Rogan leaned across her and pushed the button. "I fixed it."

As they rode up, he closed his eyes for a moment, drawing a deep breath and taking in the scent of her perfume. He usually didn't care for perfume, but right now, his senses seemed to be operating in overdrive. Everything about her was much more tantalizing than it should be. By the time they reached her room, Rogan was already wondering what it might be like to kiss her.

She had an amazing mouth, wide and expressive, with lips the color of ripe berries. He knew the unwritten rule that a guide should never seduce a client. But Claudia really wasn't a client. He wasn't guiding her, he was guiding her patients. And so was she. By all accounts, they were coworkers. At least, that was the story he was telling himself.

He pulled her keycard out of his jacket pocket and handed it to her, but she struggled to make it work.

Rogan reached for it, but she brushed him off. "I can certainly get the door open," she said.

She made an amusing spectacle, her dark hair tumbling around her face, her color high. Each attempt was followed by a soft curse. "Not so quick," he advised. "And wait for the light to go green before you pull it back out." Claudia gave it a few more tries before she reluctantly handed the card to him. "You do it."

He reached around her and unlocked the door, then pushed it open. "After you."

Claudia turned and stood in the doorway, blocking his entrance. "Thank you for everything you did. I appreciate your…efficiency."

He held out her drink. "Well, good night then."

She reached out for it, but miscalculated and ended up knocking the glass into his chest. The vodka sloshed onto his shirt and she reached out to wipe it away. Rogan captured her hand with his and pressed it against his chest, her delicate fingers splaying over the damp fabric of his shirt. His pulse quickened and his heart pounded against her palm.

"Can I ask you a question?" she murmured.

She raised her gaze to his and he fought the urges coursing through him. "Sure," he said.

"If you're thinking about kissing me, what's stopping you?"

Was that an invitation? Or a rhetorical question? He wasn't sure. But the scent of her hair and the sight of her lush, damp mouth was too much to resist.

At the same time, she was drunk and he wasn't about to do something that she'd regret the next morning.

He bent closer and brushed his lips against her warm cheek.

When he drew back, her green eyes were wide with surprise, her lips parted as if she were about to say something. He fought the urge to take things a step further. Then she threw her arms around his neck and took the decision out of his hands.

Her lips were soft and damp, and as the kiss spun out of control, Rogan smoothed his hands around her waist and drew her closer. So much for him loosening her up. She seemed more than willing to live in the moment, and this moment was surprisingly powerful.

A flood of desire surged inside him, the anticipation acute. And yet, he couldn't act on it; given her condition, it would be best to make a quick retreat.

He drew away, and before she had a chance to kiss him again or invite him inside, he gently pushed her farther into the room. "Good night, Claudia," he said, grabbing the door. "I'll see you in the morning."

He turned and stepped into the hallway, closing the door behind him. As he strode toward the lift, Rogan reviewed his last move in his mind. There was an obvious attraction between him and Claudia that couldn't be denied. But how far was she willing to go to explore it? Once sober, would she shut him down with some excuse about professional behavior? Or would she let down her hair and indulge?

He was a good guide, and he could handle whatever her patients threw his way. But Claudia was a different matter. She seemed to put him off his game, to jumble this thoughts and tease his desire. And with so much riding on the success of this trip, could he risk adding seduction to the adventure?

But was it a risk? After all, he was a master at separating sex from emotion. It wouldn't be any different with Claudia Mathison.

2

CLAUDIA WOKE TO a sharp rap at her hotel room door. She pushed up from the pillows and groaned, realizing that she'd slept in her clothes the night before. Squinting, she tried to make out the time, then cried out when she saw it was already past noon. She hadn't overslept in years. The latest she allowed herself to linger in bed was 8:00 a.m., and that was only on Sundays.

She scrambled out of bed but her legs got tangled in the sheets and she lurched toward the door, her head pounding. When she pulled it open, she found Rogan standing in the hallway. "Why didn't you wake me earlier? What's going on? Where is everyone?"

"We're waiting downstairs. Did you just wake up?"

"Of course, I just woke up," she said. "If I'd been awake earlier, I would have been downstairs on time."

"You're wearing the same clothes you were wearing last night."

Leave it to Rogan Quinn to state the obvious. "It's your fault. You gave me that last drink." She strode to the bed and began to gather her things. Then she stopped.

The events of the previous evening came flooding back into her mind. Their conversation. The way he'd touched her. The kiss. Warmth rose in her cheeks.

"I apologize, that was unfair. I was feeling sorry for myself and I drank too much. You're not in any way culpable."

"Thank you," Rogan said, glancing around the room. He reached down and picked up an empty bag of crisps. "What did you do, raid the minibar?"

"I was hungry." She stopped. "Before I go any further, I have something to say. I seem to recall that I kissed you last night. And I want to apologize if I compromised your professional integrity by doing that. I meant no disrespect."

"We both participated in that kiss," Rogan said. "And it was quite enjoyable, as I recall. Didn't you like it?"

Claudia rubbed the sleep out of her eyes. "Of course, I— Yes, it was quite lovely."

She sank down on the edge of the bed, a sudden wave of dizziness overwhelming her. Rogan had kissed her— or she had kissed him. The particulars really didn't matter. Though it had been just a brief indulgence, it had been deliciously intriguing. So intriguing that she'd spent a good hour afterward stuffing herself with snacks from the minibar as she tried, with her martini-muddled mind, to analyze exactly what had transpired between them.

"Are you all right?" he asked.

Her stomach roiled, and for a second she thought

she might be sick. Then, an instant later, she *knew* she was going to be sick. "Excuse me," she muttered as she raced to the bathroom.

The humiliation was almost more than she could bear, but there was no stopping the symptoms of a hangover. When she'd finally finished retching, she glanced up to find him watching her from the doorway of the bathroom. Claudia covered her face with her hands. "Go away!" she cried.

She heard the water running and then he was there, sitting next to her on the floor. He pressed the cool cloth to her forehead. "You look quite lovely this morning," he said.

Claudia managed a quick laugh. "Oh, I feel lovely," she replied, her voice filled with sarcasm. She tried to get up, but it was too much effort so she leaned back against the side of the bathtub. "I really didn't mean what I said," she murmured. "You've really been quite wonderful. And I've been an utter mess. You must think I'm a first-class loon."

"No, I think you're quite wonderful, as well," Rogan said.

"I can take the truth," Claudia said. "I specialize in the truth."

"I've noticed that about you," Rogan said. "You always say exactly what's on your mind. I like that about you." He smoothed the cloth over her cheeks and lips. "So tell me the truth," he said.

"About what?"

"Would you like to kiss me again?"

She knew she ought to lie, to say that another kiss

would be wholly inappropriate. And in a corner of her soul, she realized it could only lead to disaster. Her whole career rested on her reputation, and that meant she'd had to be scrupulous about her professional behavior.

And that was even more true now. If there was even a whiff of impropriety about her, it could jeopardize any thoughts of an academic career. If the hiring committee had even the slightest concern about her conduct, they could put her at the bottom of the list.

And yet, didn't she deserve to have a personal life, one that included excitement and passion? How could she possibly convince her patients to live in the moment when she didn't do the same?

If it was just about her, she might consider it. But her father was getting older and as time passed, he'd need even more help and financial support.

Claudia cursed herself inwardly for once again analyzing everything to death. It was just a kiss. It wasn't as if she planned to jump into bed with him.

"If it's taking you this long to answer, you must have reservations," he murmured. "I take back the question."

She had enjoyed kissing him. And she wanted to try it again just once—after she brushed her teeth two or three times, of course. "Yes," Claudia said.

"You'd like to kiss me?"

"Yes, but not right now. Maybe later?"

"Later," he said. "I can wait."

"I need a bit of time," she said, her gaze fixed on his. "I have to figure out how to handle you first."

"I don't need handling," Rogan said. "I'm not one of

your patients." He reached over and hooked his finger beneath her chin, his eyes dropping to her lips. "I find myself strangely obsessed with your mouth. Is there a cure for that, Dr. Mathison?"

Claudia groaned inwardly. Did she possess the strength to resist him? Did she even want to attempt to maintain her distance? In all honesty, the trip was already a disaster and her career was probably already ruined. What could possibly make it worse?

When his gaze finally rose to her eyes, Claudia knew she was fighting a lost cause. She was in a weakened state, her confidence flagging, and when he turned his charm on her, she felt so much better about herself.

If one of her patients had said that to her, Claudia probably would have warned her off, explaining that she could become dependent on a man to validate her self-worth. But right now Claudia didn't care. Rogan could validate all he wanted.

"I should probably go check on the group," Rogan said. "After I told them what we were going to do today, they seemed a bit anxious."

"What are we doing?" Claudia asked.

"I've arranged a kayaking trip down Puhoi River. It's smooth water and just eight kilometers. Plus the tide pulls you along so it isn't too difficult physically. And the scenery is beautiful. I think everyone will enjoy it."

She groaned softly, the idea of spending the day on a boat causing another wave of nausea. "It sounds… lovely."

"If you'd prefer to spend the afternoon here, you can join us later."

"No, no," Claudia said. "I want to come. I need to come. I have to be there to observe and evaluate."

"All right. I'm going to give you a few minutes to get yourself together and we'll be waiting for you in the lobby." He got to his feet. "Are you sure you're going to be all right?"

"Yes," she said. "I'll just grab a little something to eat and then I'll be as good as new."

"We have reservations for lunch at a local pub in another hour. Great food. You'll love it."

"You think of everything," she said.

"That's my job, Dr. Mathison."

He left the bathroom and she listened for the room door to click shut behind him. She'd pictured this trip in her mind a thousand times since coming up with the plan, but she'd never imagined it would turn out like this. A rocky start, a sexy guide, a surprising kiss and a bad hangover. What was next?

"Certainly not sex," she muttered to herself as she got to her feet. She caught sight of her reflection in the mirror. "Oh, bugger." Her mascara was smudged beneath her eyes and her dark hair was a rat's nest of tangles. She peered more closely at a brown streak on her chest, then realized it was melted chocolate. She must have eaten a candy bar before passing out last night.

"Well, you've created an excellent first impression." Thank goodness her patients hadn't seen her in this state. But Rogan had. He'd seen her at her absolute worst. Maybe that was for the best. A single kiss was one thing, but encouraging some kind of relationship with Rogan Quinn was ill-advised. She had a professional reputation to maintain and if she was mooning over the handsome guide, her group would surely notice.

Besides, where would it lead? Time after time, man after man, Claudia had managed to analyze herself out of every romantic relationship that came her way. She couldn't seem to keep herself from picking apart every conversation, every simple gesture, every perceived problem until the relationship fell apart in front of her.

Though she'd tried to stop herself, she couldn't. It was one of the downsides to her profession. She knew too well how the mind worked. Claudia groaned softly, bracing her hands on the edge of the counter.

But who'd said anything about a relationship? Here was a man with whom she couldn't possibly have a future. He spent his days wandering the world, and she lived her life in an office in Sydney. If there ever was a time to indulge, this was it. It might even help give her more confidence in her work.

It felt wonderful to indulge in a bit of a flirtation and to have it reciprocated. And it didn't have to end in bed, did it? They could kiss, they could touch and then, at the end of the week, they could part. It would be simple.

And she would maintain control, as Claudia always did in her personal relationships, never allowing herself to get too far ahead of the curve, never indulging in feelings that might never be reciprocated. It wouldn't be any different with Rogan Quinn.

She quickly washed her face and brushed her teeth. Once she'd changed into fresh jeans and a comfortable cotton shirt, her outlook had improved considerably. And though she wanted to grab a shower, Claudia couldn't expect the group to wait any longer.

Grabbing her bag, she hurried to the lift and then rode down to the lobby. To her surprise, the group was relaxing on the sofas and everyone seemed calm and happy. Rogan was sitting with them but as soon as he saw her, he stood.

"There she is," he said.

"Sorry I'm late. Did you explain?"

"I told them you had an emergency call from back home." Claudia appreciated the lie. "Is everything all right?"

She sent Rogan a grateful smile. "Everything is fine. Are we ready to go? I hear we have an interesting day ahead of us."

As they walked to the van, she caught up with Rogan. "Thank you. I usually don't lie to them, but in this case, I think it was justified."

"No worries," he said.

"So what's the plan for tonight?"

"We are going to camp at the regional park at the end of our kayak trip. It's a pretty tame spot, but it will be a good test. I'm going to teach everyone a few survival skills, we'll make a camp meal and then I'm going to kiss you again. After that, my plans are pretty much up to you."

"Have you told the group?"

"About the kiss? No, but I will if you want me to."

"About your plans for them," she said.

He grinned. "I have. And though they'd prefer to stay at the hotel, they're ready for a challenge."

"It's a fine plan," she said. "Carry on."

The group had loaded their luggage into the back of the van. Rogan took her bag and tucked it into an empty spot, then he placed his hand on the small of her back as they waited for everyone to choose a seat. Claudia focused on the warmth of his hand, on the sensations caused by his touch, knowing it wasn't just a polite gesture. He wanted to touch her, to kiss her, and he was just biding his time until they were alone again.

Her pulse quickened and all the effects of her hangover seemed to disappear. She felt energized and exhilarated. She was ready to spend the day repairing her reputation as a competent therapist and getting to watch Rogan in his element.

It HAD BEEN years since Rogan had visited the quaint village of Puhoi. It wasn't the kind of place that usually popped up on his guiding itinerary. Just a bit too civilized for him and his usual clients. But for Claudia's patients, it was perfect. The town had been settled by Bohemian immigrants in the mid-1800s and retained much of its European charm.

The group enjoyed a lunch at the local pub, gathered around a long wooden table filled with food and drink. To Rogan's surprise, they were quite at ease with each other, and he came to understand that they spent every Tuesday afternoon together in group therapy, working through their individual problems.

Though Claudia hadn't given him any specific information beyond the fact that they were working on a variety of phobias, it wasn't difficult to discern what each of them was afraid of.

Emma, a tall thirtysomething woman, always had antibacterial wipes on hand, offering him his own pocket package shortly after they met. Millie, a pretty but shy twenty-six-year-old, avoided small spaces and would not use the lift or sit in a booth at the restaurant. And Leticia was afraid of heights. Marshall was a nervous forty-year-old who seemed obsessed with bugs. But Rogan hadn't quite figured out Eddie's problem yet. The skinny young man just seemed uneasy all the time.

Now on the banks of the river, Rogan stood back and watched as the group got a lesson in paddling and kayak safety by an instructor from the kayaking company. The Puhoi was a tidal river, shallow and smooth, the perfect place for novice paddlers. The presentation went without a hitch until Eddie raised the subject of crocodiles. It seemed all of Claudia's patients had heard the story of the Kiwi bloke who'd been stalked by a giant croc in Australia and were justifiably concerned.

"I can assure you," Rogan said, "that there are no crocs or snakes here in New Zealand. Except for a few spiders, we are free of creepy, crawly things."

"I hate spiders." Marshall shuddered.

"I know," Rogan replied. "But they are notoriously bad swimmers, so if you stick to the middle of the river, you'll be perfectly safe from them."

Marshall seemed mollified by Rogan's suggestion, so he moved on and spent another few minutes explaining Kiwi wildlife and its lack of any native mammal species, beyond the bat. After a long discussion about rabies and a reassurance that bats were nocturnal creatures, all five were finally ready.

As the rep from the kayaking company began to get everyone fitted for buoyancy vests, Rogan noticed that Claudia had pulled away from the group. He walked over to where she stood.

"This is wonderful," she said, her eyes bright with excitement. "They're so…engaged. And you've handled all their concerns brilliantly."

"They do seem to wind themselves up for no reason."

"You have no idea. This group has a very hard time putting their fears aside, for any reason, and they just have. Look at them. After yesterday, I would have expected to see them locked in the van, refusing to come out. But there they are, ready to paddle down a river." She turned to him. "You are a good influence on them, they respond to you. I'm not sure why, but—" .

"I barely know them. Maybe that gives me an advantage. I have no expectations."

"It might be your charm. I believe the men want to be like you and the women just want to please you. But whatever their reasons, today has been a big breakthrough for all of them." Claudia paused, then sighed. "Though, I suppose it could all fall apart at any moment. God, I hope no one tips over. You're sure there are no snakes in the river?"

"I'm sure. We'll just keep moving forward." His hand brushed against hers and for an instant their fingers tangled together. Had they been alone, in some private spot, Rogan would have taken the opportunity to pull her into his arms and kiss her. And not just a quick meeting of the lips, but a deep, raw, powerful kiss.

Why not follow his urges? His usual business as a guide required unwavering attention, especially since human lives were at stake. But this was a relaxed trip, one that he might actually be able to enjoy. And Claudia's patients were in the capable hands of the kayaking instructor.

"Come with me," he said, giving her hand a tug. "I need your help with something."

"Sure," Claudia said, following him back to the trailer.

When Rogan found a spot out of the view of the others, he slipped his hands around her waist and pulled her against him. "I'm going to kiss you again," he said. "And if you have any objection, you should say right off." He waited. "Well?"

Claudia drew a deep breath. "There are some things we ought to consider. If this is just kissing for kissing's sake, then I'm fine with it. But usually kissing comes with some expectation of further—"

He reached out and pressed his finger to his lips. "You're overanalyzing this. It's just a kiss."

Claudia moaned softly in response to his touch and Rogan drew back. Her expression was filled with confusion, her eyes wide and she drew a ragged breath.

"No," she murmured. "No objection."

He grinned, then bent close. Rogan knew there wouldn't be many more chances for this until later that evening, so he did everything in his power to make the kiss memorable.

The moment their lips touched, she opened for him, and he accepted her unspoken invitation to taste deeply and tease. Rogan had never been quite so focused on a single kiss, but this was something he'd been thinking about since last night.

Strange how first impressions could be so wrong. Over the phone, he'd considered Claudia controlling and overbearing and compulsively organized. But though she did possess those qualities, they didn't define her. Nor did they irritate him any longer. Now he was able to see her concern for her patients, her drive to help them, her goal to make everything as beneficial as possible for them.

Rogan's hands moved to her face and he molded her mouth to his, deepening the kiss until the need between them began to spin out of control. He knew the kiss had to end, but it took every ounce of his willpower to stop it. With a low groan, he pulled away, his palm still cupping her cheek. Pressing his forehead to hers, Rogan waited for her to open her eyes. And when she did, he smiled. "We'll have to continue this later," he said.

"When?" Claudia asked in a breathless voice.

"After everyone goes to bed, I reckon."

She nodded, then reached up to run her fingers through her hair. "And what about my question?"

"What question?"

"I thought we'd made a deal. A kiss for a question."

"Was that the deal? I thought you were only able to analyze me if I was able to loosen you up."

"I have to ask questions," she said.

He realized then that trying to understand people

was as much an essential part of her as her urge to help and to heal. He could not respect one without the other.

"All right. Have at it. A kiss for a question, and you better make it good."

She thought about the question for a time then smiled. "Are *you* afraid of anything?"

"No," he said.

"That's it?"

"The question called for a yes or no answer, and I answered."

"But, I—"

"You want another question, you'll have to kiss me again."

Conceding that she'd been beaten at her own game, she stepped out from behind the trailer and walked back to the group. Rogan leaned against the trailer and drew a deep breath, trying to slow the rapid rhythm of his pulse.

Glancing down at the front of his cargo shorts, Rogan realized that he'd gotten a bit more carried away than he'd thought. Cursing softly, he tried to turn his mind to something other than Claudia's naked body, writhing beneath his. But it was impossible to make the erection fade in a matter of seconds.

"Quinn!"

He peeked around the corner of the trailer to see everyone ready to launch their kayaks. "Go ahead," he called to the guide. "I'll be right there."

Rogan waited until they'd all pushed off and were practicing their paddling skills before heading to the landing, grateful that the kayak hid his reaction to his encounter with Claudia. When he finally paddled over to the group, they were already floating downstream with the tide.

He spent the first hour of the trip providing a travelogue of the surrounding landscape. Once they left the village, they drifted past farm fields and crop land. But as they wound closer to the Hauraki Gulf, the shores became thick with mangrove forests, the trees' twisted branches and trunks obscuring the river shore.

The raucous cries of a kookaburra echoed in the clear afternoon air and they glided past statuesque herons and blue-breasted pukekos. Sacred kingfishers swooped over the water, catching prey in their long beaks before retreating to the trees above.

He'd brought along binoculars for each group member and encouraged them to let the water carry them along as they watched the variety of birds in the area. While they observed the birds, Rogan took photos with a small digital camera he'd tucked into his jacket. If they planned to market these types of adventures in the future, Mal would want photos for the website. Plus, it was a rare treat on an expedition to have the chance to take photos, and he enjoyed it thoroughly.

It was a perfect day for a peaceful paddle, a slight breeze ruffling the leaves overhead and the spring sunshine warming the air. For most of the trip, Rogan focused on Claudia's patients, making sure they were comfortable. But the instructor had them well in hand, so when Rogan saw Claudia paddle over to a small inlet, he followed her.

The afternoon light caught her just right, and he

reached for his camera and snapped a few more shots. "Hey," he said as he silently glided up beside her.

"Hey," she replied, smiling.

"Everything's going well," he commented.

"Perfect."

"I got some nice photos of the group," he said, holding out the camera. He flipped through them and she smiled.

"These are wonderful. Thank you. I never thought to bring a camera. Privacy issues and all."

"Then I shouldn't take photos?"

"No. They'd probably like to have memories of this trip. A few of them brought their own cameras along, but feel free to take your own pictures." She handed him the camera, then drew a deep breath. "I think I needed this trip more than they did. It's been so long since I've truly relaxed. I can take a deep breath, and it feels so good."

"Me, too."

"But don't you do this for a living?"

Rogan chuckled softly. "On an expedition, I'm usually occupied trying to keep my clients from falling off the side of a mountain or freezing to death. This is practically a holiday for me."

"Before this trip if you would have told me I'd learn to paddle a kayak, I would've called you mad. But I'm quite proud of myself. I haven't come close to falling in."

He smiled at her, his gaze drifting down to her mouth then back up to her eyes. Now that he'd kissed her, he couldn't seem to think of anything else but her lips. He wanted to drag her into his arms and indulge in a slow, delicious seduction. But would that mean more questions to answer?

Oh, bloody hell. It wasn't as if he'd let slip anything interesting. She could bring on the Spanish Inquisition and he'd confess all his sins and she'd be bored to death. He'd been with his share of women, but not any more than other men his age. He hadn't let any of them get really close to him, and he wasn't about to start now.

Their kayaks brushed against each other and he circled around her, the boats becoming extensions of their bodies. Each time they rubbed and bumped, his desire built. Finally, when it became impossible to deny, Rogan reached over and pulled her kayak against his.

Their gazes locked, but when she shifted her weight closer, the side of her kayak dipped too low. Claudia screamed, grasping at his buoyancy vest with her free hand as she threatened to capsize them both.

Instinct urged him to push her away from him, but Rogan knew the only way to keep her upright was to grab her waist and pull her in closer. At first, she flailed with her paddle, trying to regain her balance, but when his lips came down on hers, she calmed down and managed to find her equilibrium.

"There," he said, drawing back. "That will set you right."

"Yes," she murmured, tipping her face up to look into his eyes.

Crikey, she was beautiful. The dappled light made her eyes the most brilliant color of green he'd ever seen, and her dark hair fell around her perfect face, blown softly by the wind.

As he kissed her again, his hand slipped to her bum. A tiny moan slipped from her lips as the kiss deepened and her fingers tangled in the hair at his nape.

It was a precarious seduction, hidden only by the low-hanging branches of a mangrove. Every time they moved to deepen their kiss, the kayaks rocked in response. But he held the boats tight with one arm, keeping them both upright.

"See?" he murmured, smiling down at her. "We just have to stay close. Very, very close."

"Dr. Mathison? Hello? Is everything all right?"

Rogan glanced over his shoulder to see the instructor on the other side of the mangrove. The rest of the group was paddling back upstream to search for them. "No problem," he called. "Just a minor collision." He lowered his voice. "I'm going to push off and you just sit up straight."

She did as he ordered and they drifted apart again. Rogan grabbed his paddle, which had been floating in the river beside him, then quickly spun around to face the instructor and the group. "She got herself tangled up in the roots while she was focused on watching a bird."

They seemed satisfied with the answer, though Emma gave him a suspicious look as she turned and paddled away. Rogan smiled at Claudia, then nodded his head. "And try not to get yourself tangled up again," he said, his voice echoing across the water.

"Thank you for the advice, Mr. Quinn," she replied in an overly loud tone.

She paddled past him and Rogan admired her form for a long moment. "No trouble at all," he said, his thoughts jumping ahead to the evening's activities.

"I'll count that as two questions," she said with a smile.

"You're keeping a tally, then?" He smiled. She could count his debts if it pleased her. But Rogan had no intention of spending their time together in conversation. He had other more interesting activities in mind.

THEY'D ENJOYED A wonderful camp dinner of freeze-dried beef stew and apple sauce, prepared with boiled water and eaten out of Mylar pouches. They'd hunted for edible roots and berries in the surrounding area and had tried a few selections before Rogan taught the group how to start a fire without matches.

Claudia had been amazed at how these added bits of knowledge seemed to boost each of her patients' confidence, and after dinner they all sat near the fire and practiced their newfound skills. As she sat with them, Claudia glanced over at Rogan, studying his face in the flickering light.

She was usually quite adept at reading people, but the more she observed Rogan, the more he confused her. He was so cool and competent, as if he was sure of exactly who he was and where he belonged. And yet she had a sense that there was much more to him, buried beneath the handsome facade.

They were playing a game, kisses for questions. But it wasn't some silly pastime to her. She wanted—*needed*—to know everything about this man who had swept into the midst of their dysfunctional little group and turned everything upside down.

He'd already proven that he could handle her patients— more handily than she usually could. And they all seemed to admire him, even when he pushed them to move beyond their fears. When it came from her, it sounded like nagging. But when he chided the group for their fears, they seemed to work harder to please him.

She thought this trip would give her a chance to learn from her patients, but Claudia was slowly beginning to realize that she might learn more from Rogan Quinn. She wanted to discover his secrets, both professional and personal.

She watched him as he told the group a story about a climbing trip he'd led in Nepal. They were all enthralled by the tale. But after a few minutes, Emma stood up and moved away from the group then plopped down next to Claudia.

"He's a handsome bloke," Emma whispered to her. "I like his hair. So thick. Don't you just want to run your fingers through it?"

Claudia gasped softly. "No. Of course not. Do you?"

"Only if he'd just washed it with antibacterial soap," Emma sighed.

Claudia glanced over at her in surprise.

"It's a joke. Besides, he's not really my type."

It wasn't like Emma to poke fun at her phobia. Most of the time, it seemed to consume her life. Was she seeing things differently now? And did her change of heart have to do with Rogan?

"He's not that handsome," Claudia said. "And not my type, either."

"Come on now," Emma said, "The five of us may have a few kangaroos loose in our paddocks, but we're not a bunch of boofheads. Except for maybe Eddie. Admit it. You fancy Rogan."

She shook her head. "We don't make negative comments about our fellow group members. Constructive dialogue only," she said, focusing on Emma's comments about Eddie and ignoring the one about Rogan.

"All right, here's something constructive," Emma said. "You always say we should be honest with ourselves. I suggest you do the same. We can all see the way you two are watching each other. As if you've got hot coals in your drawers."

This brought a full-fledged gasp from Claudia. Was it that obvious? Her patients were usually so preoccupied with their own worries that they barely noticed her moods. "Of course he's attractive," Claudia admitted. "I'd have to be blind not to see that. But I don't have any intention of—"

"Don't you?" Emma asked, her brow raised. "And why not? He's single, he's available, and if I weren't madly in love with Marshall, I'd have a go at him."

Claudia's eyes went wide. "You and—and Marshall?"

"Don't ask me why," Emma admitted. "And don't tell him. I haven't, and I don't intend to. I prefer to admire him from afar. After all, how could I possibly fall in love with a man who's afraid of bugs? And who knows what kind of germs he's carrying around with him."

"I admire Mr. Quinn, yes. Look at him. He can make a fire with sticks," Claudia said. "But that's all it is. Admiration."

Oh, bloody hell, what was she saying? She'd always counseled her patients to make decisions with their heads first and not let their actions be dictated by pure emotion. And yet, she was ignoring all her most firmly held beliefs when it came to this growing infatuation with Rogan. If that didn't signal trouble, she didn't know what did.

And she'd broken one of her cardinal sins—twice. She'd lied to her patients. She always told the truth, or refused to answer. But she never lied. Only the lies had to do with her personal life, not her professional life. Maybe the sin wasn't that egregious.

"You ought to go for it," Emma said.

"I could say the same for you," Claudia countered. "But we both understand that it's more complicated than that." She cleared her throat. "I'm not sure this is an appropriate conversation for a therapist and a patient to have," she said.

"All right," Emma said, pushing to her feet. "But you should know that we're all for it."

"You've discussed my relationship with Rogan with the group?"

"Of course. What else were we supposed to yack about while we drifted down the river? Our own problems? That's a crashing bore." She stretched her arms over her head and spoke to the others. "I'm bushed. I'll be going to bed, I reckon. How about the rest of you?"

As if they'd prearranged their response, they all

stood up on cue and began to profess their own exhaustion. One by one, they said good-night to Rogan and Claudia and retired to the row of tents that they'd set up earlier.

Rogan frowned as he watched them go, then turned back to Claudia. "What was that all about?"

"Don't ask me," she said. "I'm just gobsmacked they agreed on anything."

"So are you going to stay all the way over on the other side of the fire, or would you like to join me on this very comfortable log I have here?"

"I think maybe I better stay here," Claudia said.

Rogan pushed to his feet and circled the fire pit. "Then do you mind if I join you?"

She couldn't bring herself to refuse him. In truth, she'd been imagining this moment all afternoon, wondering when he'd touch her next. She'd always considered herself firmly in control of her emotions, but since she'd met him, she'd become more and more obsessed with thoughts of what could happen between them.

Even though she was aware it was completely inappropriate for her to indulge in anything improper, especially with her patients in such close proximity, that didn't stop her from wanting him. He was just so handsome and charming and…competent.

Of all his qualities, Claudia found that the most attractive. She'd dated a number of men, all of them quite successful in their chosen fields. But not one of them had displayed the casual confidence that Rogan did. He was completely and utterly in charge, and for the first time in her professional career, she didn't need to be.

And Rogan had one other thing that the men in her life hadn't possessed—a hint of danger. He was smooth and well practiced in the art of seduction. He'd managed to lure her in with a few smiles and a clever wit, against her better judgment. And Claudia knew she ought to give him a wide berth. Yet, she couldn't keep her fantasies in check.

How would it feel to be with a man like that, to finally cede control to someone else and let him determine the course of events? Sometimes, it became just too exhausting for her, trying to keep so many balls in the air at once. But with Rogan, she could set them all down and just be herself. And yet, she still had to be careful.

"What do you have planned for tomorrow?" she asked as he sat down beside her.

"Let's talk about what I have planned for tonight," he said, capturing her hand in his. He lazily laced their fingers together, staring down at his hand as if fascinated by the act.

She forced a smile. "How do you get them to listen to you? They seem almost eager to please you."

He shrugged. "Is that not normal?"

"No," she said. "In truth, they're acting very abnormal. I can't promise you that they won't show you their difficult sides at some point, but I'm just trying to sort out why you seem to have greater success with them than I do."

He pulled her hand up to his mouth and began to kiss her fingertips. "Does it really matter?"

She watched as he pressed his lips to her wrist. "Rogan, I'm not sure we can—"

"I know," he said. "I understand."

"You do?" His gaze met hers and she saw desire flare in his eyes. Or was it the reflection from the fire? Did he regret what had happened earlier?

"I realize that you have a professional reputation to protect. And that your patients seem to be under the impression that we're hot for each other."

"They said something to you?"

"Yes. In a roundabout way. And I get it. It wouldn't look right."

"Yes. I— I mean, no. It wouldn't. It might send the wrong message. I'm supposed to be here for my patients. Not to enjoy a…a dalliance with you."

"We would enjoy ourselves," he said with a grin. "That I can guarantee."

"Oh, I have no doubt about that," she agreed. "But this trip isn't about us."

"True."

"And if we did indulge our desire, it would just be sex for pleasure's sake, wouldn't it? I warn my patients about that all the time."

"About pleasure?"

"No, about having sex with someone and then being disappointed when it doesn't lead to love."

"Does sex always have to lead to love? Can't it just be fun?"

"Of course. I'm just saying that I should try to practice what I preach. I'm sure that we could have sex and manage to keep it in perspective. But that doesn't mean that we should have sex."

"You're overanalyzing again. What do you want, Dr. Mathison?" Rogan asked. "Right at this moment, what do you need?"

She thought about his question, unwilling to settle for her first answer, which involved a great deal of pashing. He was an excellent kisser. A master of the art, and the woman in her wanted to appreciate that.

But if he was that skilled at kissing, he'd most certainly be skilled at other carnal activities, too. She wouldn't be able to stop at just kissing and she wasn't in a position to indulge—at least not right now. So maybe she'd settle for a long, deep good-night snog and leave it at that. She slowly stood, then shoved her hands in her jacket pocket. "I think I want to go to bed."

"Or you could ask me your questions. By my count, I owe you at least two, possibly three answers."

"I get the sense that you won't really answer my questions."

"Oh, you do have me sorted out, don't you?"

"Maybe that's all for the better," she said. "If you don't answer questions, then I don't have any reason to kiss you again."

"And you don't want to kiss me, I can tell," he said, his voice soft and low. "I can read it all over your face. See, I've got you all sorted now."

She drew a ragged breath. "Good night, Rogan."

He stood up beside her and slipped his arms around her waist. "Then kiss me good-night," he said. "Don't analyze it. Don't weigh all the consequences or worry about what your patients might think. Just do it."

Groaning softly, she pressed her head against his chest. His fingers tangled in the hair at her nape and Claudia knew that if she gave in now, she'd be taking a step closer to the edge of a very dangerous sexual cliff.

"All right, go to bed, Doc," Rogan whispered after a long silence. "I'd tell you to sleep tight, but I doubt you'll get much rest tonight."

"Why is that?" she asked, looking up at him.

"Because you're going to spend the entire night worrying about what you should have done. How you should have taken a chance and had a little fun. How you should have done something just a bit reckless."

"You make it sound so simple," she said. "But I can't tell you how many women I counsel who, when faced with the same dilemma, made the wrong decision."

"Stop thinking like a shrink," he said.

"And start thinking like…"

"The beautiful, sexy, passionate woman you really are."

"You always say the right thing, don't you? I swear, if you were the devil himself, women would still fall for your charms."

He stepped back. "Enough excuses, Claudia. Go to bed. I'll see you in the morning."

As she started toward her tent, Claudia felt the frustration building inside her. He was absolutely right. She overthought every single decision she made, weighing the pros and cons until her mind was so muddled, she couldn't possibly make a decision. But this wasn't just a personal decision, this was also a professional one. And it would have to be enough to believe that had they been alone in the woods, she would have gladly accepted his invitation.

She could certainly handle a purely physical affair. As a trained psychologist, she knew the pitfalls and could keep herself from tumbling headfirst into them. There needn't be any emotional attachment; it would be entirely about physical release. And what would be so difficult about that?

Plenty, she mused. It was already close to impossible to control herself when he touched her. Every last inhibition seemed to escape her body the moment he took her in his arms and kissed her. She could no more control her attraction to Rogan Quinn than she could control the sunrise or the tides.

When she reached her tent, she unzipped the flap and crawled inside. They'd transferred their gear into packs, and Rogan's sister, Dana, had taken their luggage away.

They had each been given a battery-operated lamp to get them through the night. Claudia turned the torch on and examined the interior of her tent. She'd never slept outdoors before. They hadn't taken many family vacations when she was a child. Her mother had left them when she was six, leaving her father to care for her. They'd fallen into a very organized life which revolved around his work as a rare-books conservator and Claudia's education. There hadn't been much time for fun, not that her father had ever indulged in fun.

She hadn't realized there was something odd about him until she was in her mid-teens. Then she began to notice that her dad rarely left home for any reason. She did all the grocery shopping and picked up the mail, and he stayed in his shop, working on his musty old books.

When she'd asked him to come to her school activities—the science fair and her debate competitions—he had always found an excuse.

Then in college she'd taken a psychology course and everything finally made sense. Her father was agoraphobic. He was afraid to leave the house, afraid of unfamiliar surroundings and large crowds. No matter how important the event, he just couldn't bring himself to step outside the safety of his own little world. She finally understood why her mother had left, why life with James Mathison had become unbearable. And why Claudia had been left behind to care for him.

The revelations had piqued her interest in psychology. When she became a psychologist, she'd tried to help her father, but he wasn't interested in changing his life. He was happy with his books, and with the internet he was able to get almost anything he needed—including grocery delivery—from the comfort of his workshop.

Because of her father and her own interest in human nature, clinical psychology had seemed like the perfect career choice for her.

But now she'd begun to question her choice and her abilities. Maybe she'd expected too much. A therapist would naturally want to find a cure for a problem patient. But some problems were too deeply embedded to be cured. Once a person accepted their phobia as a part of a normal life, it was very hard to dislodge it.

She'd hoped for a few breakthroughs on this trip, a chance to move some of her patients forward in a new and powerful way. She hadn't been able to effect much change in their office sessions, after all. But what if she was wrong? What if pushing them out of their comfort zones didn't work? Then she'd seriously have to reevaluate her choice of profession—and her goals.

She'd hoped to keep academia an option if she wanted to step away from clinical work. But what university would want a psychologist who'd been nothing short of a failure?

She picked through her belongings, searching for the fleece jumper and pants. When she found them, she slipped out of her clothes and pulled the soft fleece over her naked body.

Instead of spending all her time mooning over Rogan, maybe she ought to focus her thoughts on her patients. She searched her bag for her notebook, and in the dim light of the torch began to scribble down her observations. And yet, even with her attention firmly fixed on her professional duties, her mind still wandered to the man sleeping in the tent next to her.

Fantasies filled her head, a flow of images so tantalizing that she didn't want them to stop. She imagined what he looked like naked, lying beside her, his arousal too much to deny. She'd crawl on top of him, straddling his hips, moving against him until there was nothing left to do but surrender.

"Bloody hell, just stop it," she muttered. "You're torturing yourself."

And yet, it didn't feel like torture. For the first time

in her life, she considered letting go completely, giving her body to a man to do with as he pleased. Rogan was probably much more experienced in the subtleties of the female orgasm than she was.

She imagined all the ways he might pleasure her, the passionate intimacies they'd enjoy on their way to their release. With a low groan, she flopped back onto the sleeping bag.

How was she ever going to get through a week without surrendering to these fantasies? And why put off the inevitable, especially when they could be enjoying all those pleasures right now? He'd called her a sexy, passionate woman. She wanted him to be right. Only he could prove it to her.

3

"ROGAN? ARE YOU AWAKE?"

Her voice was muffled through the nylon of the tent flap, but loud enough to wake him from a fitful sleep. The light from her torch seeped into the interior, and Rogan held his hand over his eyes as he pulled the sleeping bag across his naked body. "I am now. Come on in."

He was surprised she'd come. In truth, he'd done everything but send her an engraved invitation, but Claudia was the kind of woman who was very hard to persuade. She let her brain rule her body, and that was never a good thing.

When it came to romance, Rogan had lived his entire life pleasing his impulses. When he saw something he wanted, he went after it and didn't give up until he was fully satisfied. Hell, if he'd weighed the pros and cons of every sexual relationship, he'd be one very frustrated bloke.

For a moment, Claudia fumbled with the zipper, but then managed to get it open. He moved over to make a place for her to sit as she shut the flap. "Is everything all right?"

"I can't sleep," she said, settling down next to him.

She pointed the torch at him and he squinted against the glare, then gently took it from her hand. "What's worrying you? Everything went very well today."

"It's not that," she said. "I—I just felt that we ought to talk. About what's been going on between us."

"No," he said, shaking his head.

"No?"

"No. All you do is talk, Claudia. Besides, there's nothing to talk about. Either you want me or you don't. Talking about it is not going to convince you one way or the other."

"But, I believe it's always best to sort through these things before making a rash decision. If I'm really confused over a decision, I usually write down my thoughts. It helps me to visualize the outcome if I have—"

"You like listening to yourself talk far too much," he interrupted. "We're not having a conversation here, I'm just listening to you think out loud. And I'm really not interested in that right now."

"You're not interested in what I have to say?"

"Not at the moment. Not when all I really want to do is tear off all our clothes and get to it."

"Because I'm a sexy, passionate woman?"

"Exactly."

Rogan saw her gaze flit down to his mouth, then back up to meet his eyes again. She drew a ragged breath and her lips parted. It was enough for him, enough to take the chance that she wanted exactly what he did. Slipping his hand behind her neck, he pulled her closer and kissed her.

Her surrender was almost immediate. Claudia wrapped her arms around his neck and pulled him down beside her. Rogan gathered her in his arms until her body was stretched out beneath his.

Though it hadn't been that long since he'd spent a night with a woman, the desire inside him quickly burned out of control. He needed to touch Claudia, to feel her body beneath his hands, to kiss her until neither one of them could stop themselves.

He slid his fingers beneath the soft fleece of her jacket, finding nothing but warm, naked flesh beneath. But it wasn't enough just to touch. Every sense was crying out to be satisfied. Rogan slowly drew the zipper on the jacket down to her waist.

As her naked breasts were exposed to the chilly night air, Claudia shuddered. He bent close and pulled her nipple into his mouth, gently sucking until it formed a hard peak. But she wasn't satisfied to be a passive participant in this seduction. Instead, Claudia reached down to tug at the sleeping bag.

He held up the open side and she snuggled closer. But as her hand ran along his torso to his hip, she paused as if she'd just realized he was naked. "I saved us both the time," he whispered, his lips brushing against her soft hair.

Claudia smoothed her hand over his belly then down to graze the tip of his hard shaft. Rogan's breath caught in his throat and he held his breath, waiting for that exquisite moment when she'd wrap her fingers around him.

When she did, his response was swift and intense, a tremor running through him. Slowly, she began to stroke, and all his attention was focused on the feel of her fingers caressing him. Everything inside him screamed for release, but he knew that he'd have to control himself or else it would all be over too soon.

Suddenly, she stopped. When he opened his eyes, he found her looking at him. "May I ask you one question?"

"Now?" Rogan asked in disbelief.

"I'm not sure that it can wait."

He groaned softly, then reached down and gently drew her hand away. "Just give me a moment." Rogan waited until his pulse had slowed and his need had subsided. Bloody hell, what a time to start a conversation. He drew a deep breath. "All right. Ask away."

"What does this all mean? I know the repercussions of decisions like this. They can be substantial and difficult to deal with, so I just want to be clear that this is purely about sexual gratification. For both of us."

"Well, not purely," Rogan said.

"Explain," she said, sitting up beside him and pulling her jacket closed. "We should be on the same page before we proceed. In fact, tell me about your last relationship."

"Do we always have to talk about everything?" Rogan asked. "Can't we just do it and enjoy it and talk about it afterward?"

"Then tell me this. Have you ever been in love?"

"No," Rogan said.

"That didn't take much thought. Never?"

"Never," he repeated.

"Why not?"

"I haven't a clue. I just never felt it. My brother is in love. Her name is Amy. I'm not sure he was ever in love until he met her. Maybe it's some kind of genetic deficiency in our family."

"Why would you say that? What would cause it?"

"Maybe my father's death when I was just a kid. And my mother's reaction to it."

"How old were you when your father died?" she asked.

"You've asked your two questions," he said. "The inquisition is over. Now you have a choice, dear doctor. You can kiss me, or you can get out of my tent and let me sleep."

"You don't think this might be dangerous?" she asked.

He groaned. "We're not planning a military campaign, we're having sex. We're not even doing that. We're *contemplating* having sex. No one is going to die or even be injured…hopefully."

"I'm serious."

"Maybe you want to work out another deal. This time we could put it in writing, if you're that worried," he teased.

"Now you're making fun of me!"

"I'm making fun because this is ridiculous, Claudia. It's just sex. Nothing more. Just you and me getting naked and getting to know each other a lot better. But I can assure you that absolutely nothing will come of it."

"Why do you say that?"

"Because I've never had anything but short-lived relationships. I'm not capable of anything else."

"Why not?"

He groaned, shaking his head. "How am I supposed to know? That's just the way it is and has always been."

She stared at him, then drew a deep breath. "All right."

"Then take your clothes off," he said, leaning back on his elbows. "Forget everything that's running through your head and think about how good it will be between us. I promise you, it will."

"It will be good," she agreed, nodding her head. "I mean, that's obvious. Even though I'm not particularly skilled in sexual matters, it's clear that you are. That's not going to bother you, is it? I mean, if I do anything wrong, you have to promise to tell me."

"You're talking too much," he said.

"But I—" Claudia stopped herself. "Oh, all right. It's a mood killer. I'll stop talking now. Full stop."

"It does tend to be a bit of a distraction."

"Maybe we should just start all over again," Claudia said, zipping up her jacket. "I'm just going to go out and come back in. And I promise, I won't say anything."

"That would be interesting," Rogan said, smiling.

She grabbed the torch. "All right. I can do this. I've just never had sex without some kind of emotional attachment. This is all very new…and exciting. I've got all these new feelings coursing through me, and normally I'd examine them more closely. But this is probably not the time. Of course, it's not the time. Stop talking, Claudia."

Rogan cursed beneath his breath. This was not going to work. He was sure there was a very passionate woman underneath her professional facade. But she wasn't ready to toss aside her inhibitions, or risk her reputation. And now, she had him questioning the wisdom of a sexual encounter between the two of them, too.

He grabbed her around the waist and pulled her close, then gave her a long, deep kiss. When he felt the first signs of surrender, Rogan drew away. "Go back to your tent, Doc, and go to sleep. You can figure this all out tomorrow."

"But I thought you wanted—"

"I've changed my mind," he interrupted.

"Oh. I *did* do something wrong. There it is. I've ruined it." Claudia glanced over at the entrance to the tent. "I— I'll just go. Thank you."

"For what?"

"For providing me with some important insight into my own psyche. It's been very…illuminating."

He watched her leave, then with a soft curse, flopped down and threw his arm over his eyes. This was the damnedest thing. Usually sex was such a simple process. He saw a woman he liked, he charmed her into bed and they had a good time. Maybe they'd meet up again, and maybe they wouldn't.

But everything with Claudia seemed so much more complicated. What was going on between them? He was curious, too. He couldn't keep his mind off her. Even now, he was still hard and ready. Rogan rolled over onto his stomach, the friction from the sleeping bag sending a delicious rush of sensation through his body.

If he was smart, he'd turn his attention back to his job—giving the best experience to his clients that he possibly could. She'd be going home to Sydney at the end of the week. A pity, that, Rogan mused. Though she was a bit of a pain in the arse, he couldn't help but be curious about what it would take to get her to truly loosen up and be herself.

She was smart. She was sexy as hell. And she was the kind of unpredictable woman that made life interesting. And he hadn't found his life truly interesting for quite a long time.

"How's that?" Claudia reached out and adjusted one of the supports on her shelter, then stepped away to examine it. She frowned. "It's still crooked."

Rogan reached for her hand when she went to make another adjustment. "You can fuss with it all day and it's not going to be straight. It will do the job."

"I'd like it to be right," she said. "Tidy."

"It's a survival shelter made of sticks and leaves. It's not supposed to be the Ritz." He squatted down. "Crawl in. See how it feels."

Claudia did as she was told. Rogan had instructed each of them to find a proper spot in the forest and make a debris hut, first constructing a tent of branches and then piling whatever materials they could find on top. Emma had decided to turn the activity into a competition, putting Leticia and Millie on her team, and leaving Marshall and Eddie to work together on their own shelter. That had left Claudia to build her own a little ways away from the others.

"It smells weird," she said. "And there are probably all kinds of crawly things in these leaves."

"You're sounding like Marshall now," Rogan teased.

"I can see his point." When something slithered along her wrist, she screamed and scrambled out of the shelter.

She brushed the debris off her jacket and shuddered. "It is warm in there, but I'm not sure I could spend the night."

"You would if you were alone in the woods without any protection."

"Now that we've built these, what are we going to do with them? You're not going to make us sleep in them."

Rogan shrugged. "It appears that I can't make you do anything you don't want to, Doc."

Claudia turned away. "You're angry about last night," she said.

"No, not angry. Just confused."

"About what? You were wrong about my true nature."

He picked up a stick and drew a figure eight in the dirt at his feet. "All right, you be the therapist here and I'll be your patient. Maybe you can explain to me why I have such an obsession with a woman I barely know."

"*Obsession* is a very strong word," she said.

"These are very strong feelings," he replied.

"Maybe you should tell me about your past relationships. Have you ever felt this strongly before?"

Rogan chuckled softly. "I'm not sure if I should lie or give you the truth."

"I can't help you if you don't give me the truth."

"No. Never. I mean, there have been plenty of women, but I've just never had to work so hard to… you know."

"I do?"

"Get them into bed."

"Oh," Claudia said. "Well, that's it then. You enjoy the chase, and I'm—rather, this woman, is giving you a bit of a difficult time."

"No, that's not it," he said.

"It's not?"

Rogan shook his head. "No. It's something else. She's not the kind of woman I normally chase. She's really smart. And wants to talk about everything. And I like to listen to her, even though most of what she says has nothing at all to do with how I feel."

She paused, then met his gaze. "I thought you were the kind of guy who didn't talk about his feelings."

"Maybe I'm changing. Evolving. It happens." He stared down at the stick he held, scraping off a bit of bark with his thumbnail. "My brother is getting married. He's found this girl he wants to spend the rest of his life with. Don't get me wrong, she's a wonderful person and they make a great pair. But I can't help but wonder if he's making a mistake. If it's actually possible to love someone for your whole life. What happens if they stop loving you? Or if they…die?"

"Like your father?"

"Yeah," he said.

"How old were you when he died?"

"Eight," Rogan said.

"Unfortunately, love does not conquer all," she said. "My father loved my mother, but she stopped loving him and she left. I don't think he ever recovered."

"The same thing happened with my mother after Dad died. She's never gotten over it. She's never remarried. She has this unflinching loyalty to him. And I'm not even sure it's well deserved."

"Why not?"

Rogan shook his head. "Love can ruin your life."

"I can see you're a 'glass half-empty' kind of guy," she said.

"Yeah, I guess I am."

"Have you ever considered that your understanding of the situation might be altered because you were so young when you formed this opinion?"

Rogan sighed. "Sometimes I wonder how my life might have been different if my father hadn't died. I wonder if I would have gone to university and taken another career path."

"Don't you enjoy what you do?" Claudia asked.

Rogan shrugged. "How can I be sure? I have nothing to compare it to. But I think I do it because I hope my dad would have approved. He used to take us out on adventures when we were kids, and I could see how much it meant to him that we liked something that was important to him. That's when we were the happiest, as a family. But now, it's a weight on all of us—at least on me. We're working so hard to make the business a success that it's not fun anymore."

"But you're great at it," Claudia said. She usually followed up a question with another question, never offering opinions of her own. But Rogan wasn't a patient.

He shook his head again, visibly withdrawing. "I should go check on the others."

"We can talk about this another time," she suggested.

"No, you don't want to try to untangle the mess that's inside my head. Trust me on that."

"I thought you told me you were a normal guy."

"I guess I'm not."

"I wouldn't mind giving it a go," Claudia said.

"Are you saying I need a shrink?"

"I'm a therapist," Claudia said. "Not a shrink."

"I don't need a therapist, either. Besides, if you were my therapist, we couldn't sleep together."

"Good point," she said. "But just because we're sleeping together, doesn't mean we can't talk. I can just listen and not analyze."

Their impending sexual relationship was purely hypothetical at this point, and Claudia was beginning to wonder if it would ever progress beyond talking.

"If we ever sleep together, the last thing you're going to want to do is talk." He sent her a devilish smile, then pushed to his feet. "Come on, Doc. Let's go check on the rest of the group. I'm afraid Marshall might be bugged out by now."

"All right."

He took her hand, slipping his fingers between hers. Then he pulled her into his arms for a quick kiss. But once their lips touched, there was nothing quick about it. Claudia felt need rise inside her, and in the quiet of the woods, they were free to enjoy the encounter.

His hands roamed freely over her body, slipping inside her jacket, then beneath her shirt until he found warm, soft skin. Claudia was surprised at how easily they fell back into intimacy. Every time he kissed her, she was more certain that it would happen again, and less determined to stop him.

What had changed? Was she more certain that they could keep their feelings from spilling over into her professional life? Or did she simply not care anymore? He was gradually wearing her down until she had no defenses left.

Claudia groaned softly. "What are we going to do about this?" she murmured.

"You're going to meet me right here, tonight. After everyone goes to sleep. And it's either going to happen or we're going to stop thinking about it. Time to make a move, Doc."

"I'm not spending the night in this pile of leaves and twigs."

"You won't have to," he said. "Just come back here. And don't get lost in the dark."

"What if the dingoes get me?"

He nuzzled her neck. "We don't have dingoes in New Zealand."

"No snakes, no crocs, no dingoes. Are you the only animal I have to fear?"

"You don't have to be afraid of me, Claudia."

"I'm not afraid of you. I'm afraid of me," she said.

As they walked back to their campsite, Claudia tried

to reconcile her feelings with the doubts plaguing her mind. It wasn't that she didn't want to enjoy a night naked in his arms. She just wanted it to be perfect, something so memorable that she'd never, ever regret it.

Sex was a complicated affair at best and a tangle of doubts and insecurities at worst. And Claudia sensed she had one chance to get it right. At the end of the week, she wanted to go home with a memory of Rogan she could savor again and again. But would she analyze every last bit of fun right out of it? Or could she finally allow herself to surrender to the passion he claimed was already part of her nature?

"WHERE ARE WE GOING?" Claudia whispered. "Slow down. I can barely see."

Rogan held tight to her hand, the light from his torch illuminating the path in front of them. "It's a surprise."

The moon shone bright above them, helping him navigate through the dark woods. Since they'd left the shelter several hours ago, his thoughts had been on just one thing—the moment he could be alone with Claudia. After a long group discussion around the campfire regarding sleeping in their survival shelters, Emma and her band had staged a mutiny and insisted they would stay in their tents instead. Though Rogan had tried to convince them to give the shelters a try, they'd refused. An hour later, after her patients finally retired for the evening, he and Claudia were finally ready to get away from camp.

Rogan had told Claudia that she had to make a decision tonight. He was tired of wondering when or if it was going to happen between them. And it seemed the longer this went on, the deeper his feelings grew. What had been discussed initially as a purely physical release was beginning to take on a deeper meaning—and that scared him.

Sex had always been about pleasure and nothing more. That worked for him, provided the proper balance in his life. But this fascination with Claudia had thrown him off his game. He'd revealed more to her in their discussion earlier than he'd ever intended. And somehow he sensed that this was not going to be an ordinary affair, no matter how long it lasted.

She'd managed to get inside his head, even though he'd done his best to keep her out. Over the course of the day, they'd talked about a variety of subjects. And though he'd suspected she'd been trying to analyze him again, he didn't really care. He'd enjoyed the conversation so much that he hadn't bothered to worry about what he told her.

"We shouldn't leave them alone," Claudia said. "What if there's a problem?"

"We won't be far," he said. "It's just over here. If they call out, we'll be able to hear them."

Rogan stopped when they came to a small clearing in the woods—another campsite. He'd spent almost two hours making it perfect, and it was. Four stout branches provided the corners for a fairy-tale arbor. He'd lashed branches together to create a latticed roof of sticks and leaves, then he'd taken some of the spare torches and set them at angles, shooting light up into the trees and creating a magical setting.

He'd spread their sleeping bags on the ground and placed one of the camp lanterns in the center. A blazing fire in the fire pit crackled and popped. It was the best he could do in rather primitive conditions, but to him, it seemed romantic.

"It's beautiful," she said in a breathless voice.

"It won't protect us from the rain, but I hope it looks nice."

"You built all this during our group session?"

Rogan nodded. "Yeah. I'm better with my hands than with my mouth." He paused. "That didn't come out quite right. I'm better at building than talking."

He led her beneath the leafy canopy and pulled her down onto the soft sleeping bags. "I don't have wine, just instant hot chocolate," he said, handing her a tin cup. He poured some out of a thermos, then he held out a bowl of dried fruit. "It's not elegant, but it was the best I could do."

"It's perfect," she said, plucking an apricot out of the bowl. "This is a very unique setting."

"I wish we could have a comfortable hotel room with a big bed and complimentary robes. But this is the best I can do for tonight."

She shivered and he wrapped his arms around her and pulled her close, rubbing his hands over her back. The night air was chilly, but the temperature barely fazed him. He was used to living in sub-zero weather. The night was almost balmy to him. But Claudia lived in a climate-controlled office for most of her day. He knew how to keep her warm....

It seemed as if it had been years since he'd kissed

her, but the moment their lips met, he instantly remembered how good it was between them. "There it is," he murmured against her mouth. "That's what I've been waiting for all day long." Claudia groaned softly as he slipped his hand inside her jacket. "Isn't this where we left off last night?" he asked.

"It is. Before I started talking." She laughed softly. "I'll stop now."

He slowly unbuttoned her blouse, pulling the flannel away so he could run his hands over the soft flesh of her breasts. Her skin was warm and soft, and the light from the fire danced across her body, creating a map for his caress.

"Are you cold?" he asked.

"Not anymore," she said.

Rogan got up on his knees and tossed aside his jacket, then tugged his shirt over his head. Claudia laughed and followed his lead, pulling off her own jacket and shirt, leaving her in a lacy scrap of a bra.

Rogan reached out and fingered the black lace. "I didn't expect it to be black," he teased.

"What did you expect?"

"Something more practical."

"Analysis by underwear? Let's see yours," she said.

"Show me the rest of yours first. Go ahead. Drop your gear."

She stood in front of him and kicked off her shoes, then skimmed her jeans over her hips. The panties matched the bra. Claudia slowly turned in front of him. "What do you think?"

"You already know. I think there's a wild woman

inside you that you keep hidden during the day and only let out at night. A woman who secretly wears sexy underwear and fantasizes about sex with adventure guides."

"More than one adventure guide?" Claudia asked. She glanced around. "Have you invited a friend?"

He growled and tried to grab her, but she evaded his grasp. "I can't believe I'm standing naked in the outdoors!" She covered her face and giggled. "What if someone comes along?"

"It's nearly midnight," he said. "No one will see us. Besides, we're just enjoying nature—and all of our natural urges. Now, come here and I'll warm you up."

"Now you," she said, pointing to his jeans. "Wait, let me guess. I'd say…plaid. Boxer shorts. Or maybe boxer briefs. Blue."

He reached down and unbuttoned his jeans, then slowly pushed them down. Her eyes went wide and he chuckled softly, kicking the faded denim aside. "Surprised?"

Her gaze drifted down his body. "You don't wear underwear?"

"I find it…confining," he said, bracing his hands on his waist. "Especially when I'm usually wearing lots of other layers to stay warm. It's just wasted weight in the pack." He slowly turned. "Now that we're both nearly naked, what are we going to do with ourselves?"

Rogan was already aroused. He didn't have to look down to see the effect her body was having on his desire. Even the chill wasn't reversing his reaction.

"I suppose, if we're going to survive in this cold, we should share our body heat," Claudia suggested.

"Great idea." He stepped toward her, and when she was within reach, he gently pulled her body to his, his stiff shaft pressing against the soft flesh of her belly. The cold air made the contact even more pleasurable. Rogan smoothed his hands over the curves of her backside as he bent close and kissed her.

He'd been waiting for this moment ever since he'd first touched her in the airport. He couldn't explain their attraction, only that it was powerful, overwhelming.

She tipped her head to the side and his lips found the base of her neck. She offered no resistance and Rogan continued to explore her body, his hand running over her hip to the soft spot between her legs. His fingers slipped over her moist folds and he began a gentle rhythm, coaxing the pleasure from her body.

He moved lower, kissing a trail from her collarbone to the cleft between her breasts. He licked the stiff peak of her nipple as he continued to caress her, and when he slipped a finger inside her, she cried out in pleasure, the sound echoing through the silence of the night.

Every sense was amplified in the cold air. The sound of the trees rustling overhead and the night birds in the brush. The damp of their tongues clinging to exposed skin, now prickled with goose bumps.

Her fingers tangled in his hair and he kissed her deeply as she arched against him. He continued his assault, sensing each time she was close to release and slowing, hoping that in the end, her climax would be deep and powerful.

Her orgasm came quickly, and before he knew it, she was shuddering against him, her fingers tangled in his hair as he softly bit her neck. When the last of her spasms subsided, he took her hand and led her over to the sleeping bags.

They stretched out next to each other, pulling the down-filled bags around their naked bodies. Rogan continued to explore, determined to touch every spot of skin before the night was over. He grabbed her hand and pressed it to his heart. "Feel that?"

"Yes," she replied.

"I can't help myself. That's what you do to me." He pulled her against him and gently kissed her again. A few seconds later, he felt her fingers wrap around his shaft. A groan slipped from his throat and he deepened the kiss, silently urging her on.

Every stroke was exquisite torture as she brought him closer to the edge. And though his thoughts were sharply focused on the touch of her fingers, he wouldn't surrender. He wanted more than this.

Rogan grabbed her waist and pulled her on top of him, the sleeping bag falling to the side. He gazed up at her beautiful body, her perfect breasts, her slender waist, the light from the lantern creating shadows against her pale skin.

She nestled against his shaft, the damp between her legs creating a tantalizing friction when she moved. Rogan wanted to slip inside her, to feel her without a latex barrier between them. But they had to keep some sense. He reached for the condom he'd tucked in the back pocket of his jeans and handed it to her.

"I think we might need this," he murmured.

She opened the package and smoothed the condom over his shaft. And as she sank down on top of him, Rogan arched into her body, her warmth surrounding him until he was completely consumed.

As she moved above him, he lost himself in the pure pleasure, trying hard to maintain control. At first, he didn't notice the raindrops that hit his bare skin. But then, they began to come more quickly, splattering against their naked bodies until their skin was slick.

The rain poured down on them, but they didn't stop. Rogan smoothed the damp hair from her face as she moved above him, her bottom lip caught between her teeth, her eyes half-closed. Droplets clung to her lashes and the rain ran in tiny rivulets over her smooth cheeks.

And then he felt his body begin the slow tumble over the edge. He grabbed her hips and drove into her once more, surrendering to the deep shudders and spasms of his release, knowing she wasn't far behind. Just then, a tiny cry tore from Claudia's throat and a moment later, she joined him, her body collapsing against his chest.

He pulled the sodden sleeping bag over them, but the cold was already seeping through. She pushed up and wiped a damp strand of hair off her face. "Where's that survival shelter when you need it?"

He chuckled, then rolled her off of him and pulled her to her feet. Wrapping the sleeping bag around her, Rogan helped her put her shoes back on. "Leave the clothes. We'll get them in the morning."

They ran through the rainstorm, laughing and stumbling, their naked legs spattered with mud. The light from the lantern guided them through the trees and back to their campsite, and when they fell into Claudia's tent in a tangle of limbs, Rogan began the seduction all over again.

He couldn't get enough of her. But it wasn't just physical. There was a deeper connection, something that refused to fade when they were apart. Rogan couldn't imagine going a day without thinking about her, without wanting to talk to her or kiss her. What did that mean?

Hell, this was all so confusing. Maybe he did need therapy. He had no idea what to do with all these strange and unfamiliar feelings. He wanted her, but then he didn't want her. He was certain it would be over at the end of the week, but then he couldn't help but wonder if there was a future in it.

He'd feared falling in love for most of his life, certain that it could only result in heartbreak. And yet he longed to experience something much deeper with Claudia than anything he'd ever had. He wanted all of this craziness to mean something in the end.

Rogan pushed the maelstrom of doubts aside as he lost himself in her body once again. There were moments when it all made sense, moments when the need was so acute or the pleasure so intense that it blocked all his fears from his mind. But eventually he returned to reality and faced the fact that he hadn't a clue as to what was happening between them.

He'd have to work it all out before the end of the week. She'd walk out of his life, and he had no intention of doing anything beyond wishing her well and waving goodbye. That was the way it had always been with the women in his life, and that was the way it would be with Claudia.

4

CLAUDIA OPENED HER eyes and groaned, her head throbbing, her throat raw. The morning light shone through the green nylon of the tent and she pushed up on her elbows. She peeked beneath the sleeping bag, surprised to find that she was wearing her fleece. Then she remembered Rogan had dressed her before he'd left at sunrise.

She pressed her hand to her forehead, wondering why she felt so miserable. The space behind her eyes throbbed and she noted the symptoms of a cold coming on. Was it any wonder? She'd been running around naked in the rain last night. Though she knew that wasn't the way one caught a cold.

She searched the tent for her shoes and found them in the corner, caked with mud. Drawing a deep breath, she unzipped the tent and stuck her head outside. The instant the sunlight hit her face, a sharp pain shot through her temple.

Rogan turned from the fire when he heard the tent open, then smiled. "Morning," he called.

"What time is it?"

"Ten, ten-thirty."

"Where is everyone?"

"They took off on a tramp with Dana. She stopped by with supplies, and I asked if she'd take them out. I didn't want to leave you alone."

"They won't get lost, will they?"

"Dana has a map of the trails. I gave the group a book on edible plants and they're collecting some. We're going to use them in our lunch." He frowned. "Are you all right?"

"I think I caught a cold. My head hurts and my nose is stuffy and my throat is sore. Is there coffee?"

He grabbed the pot from the fire and poured some boiling water into a mug, then added a spoonful of instant coffee. He walked over to the tent and handed it to her, at the last moment bending close to kiss her.

"You're going to catch my cold," she said.

"I probably caused your cold," he said. "Making you get naked in the rain and chill. I'm sorry. What can I do to make you feel better?"

She gave him a sideways glance. "You don't get a cold from being chilled. It's a virus. And it's probably from the plane. I always get sick after I fly. And it usually hits about three days after."

"Hang on," he said. "I'll be right back."

Claudia crawled inside the tent again and sipped at the coffee. It wasn't as satisfying as her triple-shot soy latte that she ordered every morning on her way to work, but it was dulling the ache in her head and warming her fingers.

When Rogan returned, he sat down cross-legged at her feet. "Here. Take your pick."

"What is this?"

"Everything you had on your list for the first-aid kit. I spent two hours at the chemist's getting it all. I think there's a bottle of cold tablets in there. And some cough syrup. I can even perform an appendectomy if it's called for." He plucked out a bottle and a few tubes. "Allergy medication? Lip balm? Anti-bacterial spray?"

"Cold tablets," she said. "Three, please. And the cough syrup?"

"Listen, after they get back from the hike and we have lunch, I've decided we'll pack up and head to a hotel. That way everyone can get cleaned up and relax a bit."

"A hot shower sounds really good right now," she said.

"I sometimes go a month without a shower."

"Oh, well, please don't think you have to prove the point for me," she said. "Shower away."

"If it would make you feel better, I could help you lather up in the shower. I can be very useful that way."

Claudia groaned again. "Don't tempt me." She reached up and smoothed her palm across his beard-roughened cheek. "I may take you up on the offer. But now, I need to get dressed."

"Yes," he said. "We'll discuss your needs later."

Though they'd finally indulged their desires, she couldn't help but wonder if she'd made a mistake. It was easy to want him and even easier to enjoy what had happened between them. But she found herself wondering how it would all end—exactly what she'd warned herself not to do.

But, in her typical fashion, she'd worked out several different scenarios, and none of them were simple. Because in truth, the notion of walking away from Rogan was fraught with complications. She couldn't just pretend that nothing had happened, or that he was just an ordinary man, not worth a second thought.

Something had shifted inside her. It wasn't anything she could put into words, but she knew for certain that he was the cause of it. She wasn't thinking of all the reasons they shouldn't want each other. Instead, she was focused on the pleasure he gave her, the feel of his hands on her naked skin, the taste of his kiss, the weight of his body on hers. She'd wanted him to prove that she was a passionate woman, but she hadn't been prepared for the consequences.

"We'll *discuss my needs?* So now you want to talk?" Claudia asked.

"Yeah," he said. "Since you've come down with a case of the dreaded lurgy, I'll have to hold off on any thoughts of seduction."

"Probably for the best," she murmured.

Rogan crawled out of the tent and Claudia closed her eyes, drawing a deep breath. "Now he wants to talk." She couldn't deny the powerful attraction between them anymore. And she wondered how far it would go if they lived on the same island and didn't have a body of water separating them.

But she reminded herself of the allure of physical pleasure. There was a purely physiological reason for this attraction, for their need for connection. He didn't want her, he wanted the rush of endorphins that raced through his body when he was aroused. That rush, those chemicals, were still clouding his brain and making him think there was something deeper between them. As soon as that wore off, he'd realize what she already knew—there was no future for them.

She'd studied all of this at university. There was no mystery to sexual attraction. It was all just a physiological response to anticipated pleasure. And yet, that didn't explain how Claudia was feeling right now. When she was with Rogan, she was a better version of herself—stronger, smarter, even more beautiful. All the flaws she usually found in herself suddenly didn't matter, didn't exist.

She didn't feel like a failure as a lover, or a daughter. There was a power pulsing through her, like a drug, and it made her invincible. And like a drug, it was proving very addictive.

But an addiction to Rogan Quinn would be like any addiction—it could consume her life, make her irrational. She was already at a crossroads professionally, falling in love with a bloke like Rogan would only make her decisions harder.

No, it was best that they call an end to their little adventure at the close of the week and go on with their lives. She drew a deep breath. But then, what if the trip was a success? Wouldn't she want to bring another group on an adventure? And who better to guide them than Rogan Quinn?

Claudia felt a sneeze coming and searched through

the first-aid box for a tissue. In the end, she found a package of Emma's antibacterial wipes. Staring down at them, she laughed. Maybe she *should* have used these on the plane. Emma certainly wasn't falling victim to a cold.

By the time Claudia got dressed, the group had returned. When she emerged from her tent, they were sitting around the fire. Claudia stopped short when she noticed everyone was wearing a surgical mask.

She sent Rogan a questioning look and he smiled weakly. "I told them you were under the weather. Sorry."

Claudia then glanced over at Emma. "I have a cold, not the plague," she said.

Emma held out a fresh mask. "You should wear this. Then we won't have to. And here," she said, holding out a huge bottle of hand sanitizer. "Most colds come as a result of touching your mouth or your nose. That's why the combination of the mask and the gel works well."

She grabbed the offered mask and shoved it on. "All right, all of you, take off the masks. Right now. Take them off."

Rogan gave her smile, but she shook her head emphatically. She was in no mood to be placated. "Have I helped any of you? It seems like in the two years we've known each other, your problems have only gotten worse, not better. I haven't helped you conquer any of your fears. I hoped this trip might shake things up a bit. But then I wake up to find you all are wearing masks. Maybe all of you need a change. Maybe we just need to go home and you can all find yourselves another therapist." She straightened. "Mr. Quinn, I think we're going to call an end to this. If you could make arrangements to take us back to Auckland, we'll catch the next flight to Sydney." She felt a tickle on her nose and she sneezed.

"Claudia, I'm not sure they—"

She turned and glared at Rogan, annoyed that he'd chosen this moment to offer his opinion. She was in charge of the group, not him. They were her patients and if she wanted to toss them all in the Tasman Sea, then she had every right.

"Sorry," he murmured, holding up his hand.

She tossed the mask on the ground. "I've been patient with all of you, trying to work with you to get over your fears. But there are moments when I wonder whether you really want to change. You seem content with the way things are. And if that's the case, what are we doing here? I can find a better use of my time, and I'm sure you can, as well." She paused, fighting back a flood of tears. "I'm going to pack. I suggest the rest of you do the same."

With that, Claudia spun on her heel and walked back to her tent. She crawled inside and zipped the flap, then sat silently, trying to figure out what had just happened.

She'd never lost her temper with her patients. Her calm objectivity was crucial to maintaining the proper tone between psychologist and patient. But she'd just let her emotions spill over into her professional life. And it had nothing at all to do with the masks or the hand sanitizer. It had everything to do with how she felt about Rogan.

"Dr. Mathison, may I have a word?"

She groaned when she heard Rogan's voice. "Go away. I just need a bit of time to myself."

He unzipped the tent, then squatted down to peer inside. "Don't you think you were a bit harsh?"

"Yes. They didn't deserve that."

"I meant you were a little harsh on yourself. They're all pretty upset. I think they blame themselves for you believing you're a failure as a therapist. They want you to come back out—without a mask on."

"No. I *am* a failure. I've worked with them for two years. And nothing has changed. They should find a new therapist."

"But they're comfortable with you."

She ran her hands through her tangled hair. "And that's the problem. I haven't been strong enough to help them. I haven't pushed them hard enough." She groaned, then pressed her hand to her head. "I may have a fever. And my head feels like it's about to split in two."

"The trip isn't over yet. Give them a chance, Claudia. They may prove you wrong. And to be honest, I think they're having fun. At least as close to fun as that group can have. And I have a good trip planned for today."

"You're just saying that because you don't want me to go home," Claudia muttered. She glanced up at him through watery eyes. And she *didn't* want to go home. But it seemed that the more time she spent with Rogan, the more she realized that she wasn't a very good psychologist. "What are we doing?"

"You'll find out when we get there."

"No, I mean what are *we* doing? You and I?"

He grinned and shrugged. "Like I said, we'll find out

when we get there. It's going to be fun. And challenging. Now pack up. We leave in a half hour." He leaned forward and kissed her, furrowing his fingers through the hair at her nape as he teased at her tongue.

"You're all right, then?"

Claudia nodded. Maybe it had been lack of sleep, or the raging headache? Or long-held professional insecurities that had bubbled up inside her. She really wanted to forget her outburst and try to move beyond it. She owed her patients an apology. They'd finish out their week in New Zealand and then they'd return home. If there were any major decisions to be made—about her professional or her personal life—she'd make them once she was back in Sydney.

EVEN IN THE midst of a head cold, she still managed to look beautiful. Rogan stood in the hallway outside Claudia's hotel room, a carton of soup and a cup of hot tea in his hands.

After packing their gear up, they'd made the drive to Matamata. Rogan had called ahead to a quaint little hotel in the center of town so their rooms would be ready. He made sure Claudia was checked in first, then sent her up to her room to get some rest while he took care of the group. Then he'd headed for the kitchen.

"Is that for me?" she asked as she opened the door, dabbing the tissue to her nose.

"It is. I hear it's magic soup. It's supposed to cure everything that ails you. I was going to get the aphrodisiac soup, but I thought you might need this more."

She took the cup of tea from his hand. "Thank you."

Claudia peered out into the hallway. "Where is everyone?"

"They're on a trip to Hobbiton. Eddie was talking about the *Lord of the Rings* movies last night and didn't realize one of the locations for the film was here in Matamata. I arranged for a driver for them."

"And where does that fall on the list of survival skills?"

"They're going on their own, Claudia. It's like a theme park. They're not in any danger and they have to venture out occasionally. And Eddie seemed to enjoy being in charge, so I figured it would be a good experience." He paused. "I think they also feel bad about the mask thing and wanted to give me time to smooth things over with you."

"I'm sure they'll enjoy the trip much more than they enjoy spending time with me," she grumbled.

"Oh, now there's a girl who needs a big dose of soup and sympathy," Rogan teased. "Why don't you crawl back beneath the duvet and I'll bring you that soup. Would that make you feel better?"

She stepped aside and he walked into her room. She followed him, then got back into bed, pulling the covers up around her chin. "When are they supposed to return?" she asked as she let the tea warm her hands.

He shrugged as he set the sack down on the desk. "They're going to find dinner on their own and then they're going to do a *Lord of the Rings* movie marathon in Marshall's room. They'll be busy all night, I expect."

"I suppose it's for the best," she said.

"This is what they need now. I think they're all afraid

you're going to stop being their therapist so they're trying to act as normal as possible. I must say, it's a bit strange."

"I was frustrated earlier," she said. "I should probably talk to them and explain."

"I suspect if they wanted to talk about it, they would have said something to you in the van on the way here. Instead, they talked about everything *but* the masks. And you didn't bring it up."

"I fell asleep," she said. "Besides, I wasn't sure what to say."

He brought the container of soup over to the bed and handed her the spoon, then sat down beside her. "Did you ever consider that maybe there's a good reason they don't want to get better?"

She frowned. "What do you mean by that? Why would they pay me if they didn't want to solve their problems? It would be a horrible waste of money."

"They seem to enjoy being with each other," he said. "They're like a little family. If they get better, that family falls apart."

She pondered his suggestion for a long moment, a frown furrowing her brow. "I suppose you could be right. But nothing is keeping them from being friends outside the office. They don't see each other now on a social basis even though they could."

"They've been forced together on this trip," he said. "It's the first chance they've had to see what it might be like to get together outside of group sessions."

"That's my fault," she murmured. "I felt more comfortable dealing with them at my office."

"And maybe you enjoy seeing them every week, too. Maybe you'd miss them if they stopped coming?"

She opened her mouth, then snapped it shut, grabbing the spoon from his hand. "As a therapist, I have to maintain my objectivity," she said. "I can't be friends with them."

"Then why did you get so upset over the mask thing?" he asked.

"I'm the one who's supposed to ask the questions, not you."

"Can I make a suggestion?"

"Can I stop you?"

"You have great instincts—trust them. Sitting around talking about their problems wasn't working, so you decided to try something new. You invited them to see their lives as an adventure. Don't give up so quickly."

Tears filled her eyes and he reached out and cupped her cheek in his hand. "Hey, come on. Don't get all weepy on me."

"Chin up," she said with a laugh. "That's what you said to me in the airport." Claudia took a ragged breath. "Maybe I should just turn my practice over to you."

"Or maybe you should realize that your instincts were right."

When she'd finished half the carton of soup, Claudia handed it to him, then curled back under the covers, pulling the duvet up to her nose. "Did you ever wonder if maybe you're not doing what you're supposed to be doing?"

"Lately? All the time," Rogan admitted.

"Why don't you try to do something else?"

"It's kind of complicated. I work for a family business, so the rest of the family is dependent on me to do my part. If I quit, it creates a burden on the people I love. So I stay."

She stared at him for a long moment, a pensive expression on her pretty face. "What would you do if you weren't a guide?"

"I don't know. I've always wanted to just take off and travel. To see new places, to experience new people. I've always enjoyed photography and I've had a few photo essays from our climbs published in outdoor magazines. If I could escape, I'd learn a little more about photography and find out if I could make a living at it."

"Really? Would you show me some of your photos?"

"A lot of them are on our company website."

She grabbed her bag and pulled out her iPad, then held it out it to him.

Rogan kicked off his shoes and tossed his jacket on the floor, then logged on to the hotel's wireless internet. When he found Max Adrenaline's website, he opened the photo albums and selected the first photo, a picture of an Argentinean farmer who he'd met on a trip to Aconcagua.

Over the next hour, he flipped through the photos, describing each one to her in detail. She curled up beside him in the bed, her head resting on his chest, the scent of her hair teasing at his nose. Rogan couldn't remember the last time he'd felt this content. With Claudia, he could open his heart and talk about his dreams, about his doubts. There was no fear or shame in admitting that he wasn't sure where his life was headed.

Hell, he was twenty-eight years old. By now, he should have figured out what he wanted. But she wouldn't judge him. Rogan kissed the top of her head and she snuggled closer. He wanted this, of that he was certain. This easy comfort that they'd found in each other.

Rogan had never experienced anything like it before, had never wanted a woman to know every thought that was running through his head. "I'm glad we have the whole afternoon in front of us," he said.

"Maybe this trip won't be a complete disaster after all."

"It isn't a disaster," Rogan said, brushing his lips against hers.

"No, it isn't," Claudia agreed.

"Is there anything I can do to make you feel better?"

She held up her hands. "You can massage my hands," she said. "My mom used to do that when I was sick. It's one of the few things I remember about her. It always helped."

He took her right hand and began to gently knead his fingers over her palm. "Tell me about your parents," he said.

She closed her eyes and sighed softly. "I'm supposed to ask the questions," she repeated.

"Just answer this one," Rogan said.

"My father is an expert in rare books. My mother… well, she left when I was six. She was too young when she got married and my father had some problems. He's agoraphobic. He hasn't left home in…well, a long while."

"Doesn't he have to work?"

"He works from home. Everything comes to him. He used to travel to authenticate rare manuscripts for museums and collectors, but that stopped around the time my mother left. He's always wanted me to take over the business. Maybe I should. He's taught me everything he knows. Maybe I'd be better with old books than phobic people."

"And what about your mother?" he asked.

"I haven't seen her since the day she left. She's living in London now and she's been married two or three more times. She's kind of a mess. I think if she came back into my life, I'd just want to fix her and I'm not sure that's even possible. And it would really hurt my father if I met with her. I think he still loves her."

"You worry about other people's feelings so much that you don't have a chance to focus on your own. How do you feel? What do you want, Claudia?"

"Right now?"

He nodded.

"Could you massage my feet?" she asked.

Rogan chuckled, then threw the covers up and over his head. "No problem," he said. "But first I'm going to have to find them."

He snatched up her foot and kissed it, and she laughed, grabbing at him until she pulled him along her body. When he was lying on top of her, Rogan smoothed the dark waves out of her face. She was so beautiful, so alluring. He loved looking at her, watching the play of emotion across her face, seeing the laughter in her eyes.

"Do you know what I'm afraid of?" Rogan murmured as he stared down at her.

"You're not afraid of anything."

"But I am. I'm afraid that you and I aren't going to have nearly enough time together." He kissed her softly.

It was more than that, though, Rogan mused. He was afraid that he might never meet a woman who made him feel the way Claudia did. For the first time in his life, he'd found a woman who…fit. It seemed as if he'd known her forever and better yet, that she'd known him just as long.

He couldn't spend enough hours with her, and when they weren't together, he found himself thinking about her, replaying everything Claudia had said or done. He wanted to confess all his most private dreams and fears to her, to be completely open and honest. But more than that, he wanted to believe there was a future for them beyond the end of this trip.

Was this what it was like to fall in love? Rogan wondered. He needed to know, yet he was afraid of the answer. He'd never wanted to fall in love, but maybe there was no way to stop himself.

CLAUDIA FELL ASLEEP wrapped in his arms and when she woke up, the fading sun had cast the room in a soft light. She stared at Rogan, studying the details of his face. He looked younger, almost boyish, when he slept.

He really was perfection, and not the type of man who usually found a woman like her attractive. Most of the men she dated were intellectuals, men whose brains, rather than their bodies, paid the bills. She'd never imagined dating any other type.

But Rogan was so strong, so physical, that he erased whatever preconceived notions she had about her "type." He made her feel as if she was the most brilliant, beautiful, passionate, captivating woman on the planet. And Claudia had never felt that way before.

She ran her fingers through his hair, brushing it off his forehead, and he stirred. He opened his eyes and smiled. "Sorry," he murmured. "I fell asleep."

"So did I," she said.

"Are you feeling any better?"

"Much better. It must have been the soup. The magic soup."

He chuckled softly. "I guess so."

"What do you think they're doing?" Claudia asked.

"Who?"

"The group?"

He growled softly, then pulled her on top of him, settling her hips against his. "Stop worrying," he said. "We have the entire evening to ourselves. I say we should take advantage of it."

"Oh, I'm going to take advantage," Claudia said. She sat back, her knees resting on either side of his thighs. Reaching for the hem of her T-shirt, she tugged it over her head and tossed it over her shoulder.

"Oh, my," he murmured. "You are feeling better."

"And how are you feeling?" Claudia teased as she unbuttoned his shirt.

"Like I should have taken these clothes off before I crawled into bed with you."

"I can help you with that," she said. She pulled him up and stripped off his shirt, then dragged him up to stand beside the bed. He kicked off socks, then skimmed his jeans over his hips. As always, he hadn't bothered with underwear, and the moment he discarded the jeans, he was naked and aroused.

"You are beautiful," she murmured, sitting on the edge of the bed and letting her gaze drift across his body.

"Not nearly as beautiful as you are," Rogan said.

"You don't have to flatter me," she murmured.

Rogan took her hand and pulled her into his embrace. "I'm not. I can't stop looking at you. I try, but whenever we're together, I just want to stare."

Claudia leaned into him and brushed a kiss across his lips. "It's just a physiological reaction," she said. "Nothing more."

"Like this?" he asked as he cupped her breast in his hand. Rogan flicked his thumb over her nipple until it puckered into a stiff peak.

"Yes," she whispered.

He ran his palm along her belly and slid his hand inside her knickers. "And this?" he asked, slipping a finger inside her.

Her breath caught in her throat and then she moaned softly. "Yes."

He twisted his fingers through the lacy scrap of her panties and tugged them down, pressing a trail of kisses from her breasts to her belly. When he was kneeling in front of her, Rogan gently pushed her back onto the bed and parted her legs.

Claudia knew what was coming, but the pure pleasure that washed over her was enough to steal the breath from her body. Her fingers tangled in his hair as he teased her with his tongue.

She expected to feel insecure or inhibited, and she waited for those feelings to come. But when he touched her body, she felt beautiful, perfect, as if she was everything he'd ever need. And she was left wondering why it was so easy to let go with him.

Tonight he was relentless, drawing her closer and closer to the edge, then pausing until she regained control. Her pulse raced, her fingers and toes tingled in anticipation. She wanted to surrender but Claudia knew that it would be a powerful release and she wouldn't be able to control it once it began.

The orgasm built within her and every nerve in her body began to hum with need. She resisted as long as she could and then gave herself over at the first spasm. Her body jerked against him and she cried out, the waves of pleasure overwhelming her.

Claudia wasn't sure how long it was before she was able to form a rational thought. But when she opened her eyes, he was beside her on the bed, his elbows braced on the edge, his gaze fixed on her face.

She reached out and furrowed her fingers in his hair, pulling him in to a kiss. And then he scooped her up and tucked her beneath the covers, crawling in beside her. "I hear that a good orgasm is a cure for the common cold," he whispered.

Claudia laughed. "Then we'd better give you a dose, as well. I'm sure I'm still contagious."

He threw his arms out on the bed. "I'm ready for the cure, Dr. Mathison."

"Well," she said. "First, there's this." She pressed her lips to his chest, then moved to the base of his throat, then to his ear. "And then, there's this."

Her fingers closed over his shaft and she slowly stroked him. He turned to her, his nose bumping against hers. "You have a lovely bedside manner, Doc."

They teased and caressed, exploring each other's bodies until there was no spot left untouched or untasted. It was as if the world had stopped spinning and they had endless time to spend in this bed. And though Claudia knew there would be an end to this adventure, it was still days away. She would take pleasure where she found it, in the present, and not think about the future. It was the perfect way to spend a lazy afternoon, and when playful kisses turned urgent, Rogan handed Claudia a condom. He watched as she sheathed him, then gently pulled her beneath him. She held her breath, waiting for that moment when he slipped inside her, that exquisite joining of their bodies and minds.

She shifted beneath him and Rogan pulled her leg up against his hip, burying himself to the hilt. As he began to move, Claudia tried to commit every sensation to memory. There would soon be a day when this would only be a part of her past, and she wanted to know that it had been real and not some figment of her imagination.

With every stroke, he teased at her need and she closed her eyes and focused on the spot where their bodies were joined. Though Claudia understood the science behind her every response, she'd never really experienced the true power of a perfect sexual encounter.

But as he drew her closer and closer to the edge, she realized that it might be possible to join him, to experience release together. As if he sensed her thoughts, Rogan rolled her over on top of him, never breaking their connection.

He ceded control to her and she set a slow pace, her hand pressed against his chest, her eyes closed. Her body was awash in pleasure, incredible sensations making every movement more exquisite than the last. But it was only when he touched her in that exquisite place that the wave threatened to drag her beneath the surface.

Her body reacted as it had each time she'd been with him, and her last ounce of inhibition disappeared. Her body tensed, then dissolved in another orgasm, this one deeper, more powerful than the last. She was barely aware of his own release but when his hands clutched at her hips, she knew he'd found it.

After the last spasm had subsided, Claudia collapsed against his chest. Rogan wrapped his arms around her and held her close, his breath warm against her forehead. When she shifted, he groaned, holding her still.

"I'd say we made good use of our afternoon," he said.

"We've cured the common cold," she said.

"Maybe we ought to try for the flu next," he said. "I'm feeling a bit feverish."

She pushed up and pressed her hand to his forehead. "You are flushed. I prescribe at least four more hours in my bed."

"Only four?"

"All right, six." She sighed. "I wonder how the group is doing?"

"Stop worrying. I gave them a mobile and told them to ring if they ran into problems. There's a little inn on the grounds so they're probably going to get dinner there before heading back."

"You really have been a wonderful guide," she said. "Very…flexible."

"You like flexible men?" he asked.

"I like you," she said. "I never expected this, but I'm happy it was you who met us at the airport."

"Me, too," he said. "You would have had a horrible time with Mal. He's engaged. And Ryan is a bit shy with women. He doesn't say much."

"Neither did you," Claudia replied. "Until I got you to start talking."

He smiled at her and her heart warmed. How was it possible to feel this sure about a man after knowing him for only a few days? It was mad. And were she both patient and doctor, Dr. Claudia would warn Infatuated Claudia to proceed with caution, to protect her heart until she was certain that her feelings were reciprocated. But she was through overanalyzing her relationships. Instead, she would enjoy every moment of it, whether it was fated to end well or to end badly.

For the moment, she was blissfully happy, and she'd deal with the consequences later.

5

ROGAN'S MOBILE WOKE him from a deep sleep. Claudia stirred beside him, the pushed up on her elbow. "What is it? Is it Eddie?"

He stared at the screen, then dropped the phone on the floor beside the bed. "Nothing. Just my brother Mal."

"Oh, good," she murmured. "I thought it might be the group. Should we check up on them?"

"They should be in the midst of their movie marathon," he said. "I'm sure they won't want to be disturbed."

"Perhaps we should join them. I feel a bit guilty spending the entire evening with you."

"Truly?"

"No, not truly," she said. "But I'm sure I'm *supposed* to feel that way." She reached over him and picked up the phone. "Maybe you should ring your brother back."

"I already know what he wants to talk about," Rogan said, "and I'm not in the mood right now."

"Are you and your brother at odds over something?"

"Someone," Rogan said. "My father, specifically."

She sat up, crossing her legs in front of her and pulling the sheet up beneath her naked breasts. "I'm going to use one of my questions. One of my sixty or seventy questions I've now accrued by kissing you so many times."

"Hang on!" Rogan said. "I didn't realize we were still counting."

"We are. And I must say, I've held up my end of the bargain." Claudia wiggled her arms. "I'm most definitely loose. And all due to you."

"Well done me," Rogan said. "All right, one question."

"You said your father died when you were eight years old. What is there to talk about now?"

The last thing Rogan wanted to do was open up the can of worms that was his family history. With every fact he revealed to her, she would only have more questions. And Claudia had earned the right to ask plenty of those. "Yes, he died in a climbing accident on Everest. He was forced to spend the night near the summit and there's really no way to survive that."

"Oh, no." She reached out and took Rogan's hand, clutching it to her chest. "Then he died quite tragically."

"He did. And he was well-known in the mountaineering community. And very successful for his young age. He was only thirty-six when he died."

"And what is it that your brother wants?"

Rogan stared at her for a long moment, wondering at the wisdom of telling her the whole story. But then, what was the difference? It wasn't anything she couldn't read on the internet. And it was part of who he'd become, both as a man and a guide.

"Some climbers found his body in April and now there's this big push for me and my brothers to mount an expedition to retrieve his effects and perform some sort of memorial to him. But it's turned into this… production. Mal is all for it, I'm against it and, for now, Ryan is stuck in middle."

"And your mother?"

"She seems to be warming to the idea, only because she thinks it would be good for us—or Mal has convinced her that it will."

"But you don't?"

"I really don't want to talk about this," Rogan said. He'd already revealed too much. Tossing back the duvet, he got out of bed and began to collect his clothes, which were scattered around the room. "I'm going to go check on the group. And I have to make some arrangements for tomorrow."

"Don't go," Claudia said. "We don't have to talk about it if you don't want to."

"No, it's fine," he said. "I just have some details to work out." Rogan stepped into his jeans, then grabbed his mobile and shoved it in his pocket.

"You seem angry," she murmured.

"I'm not," Rogan snapped. He took a deep breath. "I'm not," he said in a measured tone. "It's just a very complicated story, and one that I don't want to get into at the moment."

Though, she was a psychologist; maybe she could

help. If he told her his dilemma, that he alone held the secret of his father's possible infidelity, maybe Claudia would have an idea of how to navigate through the minefield that had been made of his father's memory. But his family had always kept their problems to themselves, and Rogan felt the need to protect them surge inside him. It was one thing to talk about himself. It was another to air his family's dirty laundry.

"It's nothing," he said, reaching out to take her hand.

"I don't believe you," Claudia replied, searching his gaze as if she could read his mind.

"Sometimes it's better to leave the past in the past."

"Better for you?"

"Better for my whole family," Rogan said.

She smiled and shrugged. "I can't help you if you won't talk to me."

"I don't need a therapist," he said.

"I'm not your therapist, I'm your friend, Rogan."

"Is that all we are?" Rogan asked.

Claudia frowned. "I'm not sure what you mean."

"What are we doing here, Claudia? Is this what friends do?"

"I thought we'd—"

"I know what you thought. That this would be very simple. And very short. But now you want to talk about my family and my father's death and you want to make it all much more complicated."

"Now you *are* angry, and I still don't understand why."

"Neither do I," he muttered. Rogan glanced over his shoulder and found her watching him, wide-eyed, her hair tumbled around her face, the sheets pulled up to her chin. Regret pierced his heart at the vulnerability in her eyes. But it was time to retreat.

He'd allowed himself to get caught up in the fantasy but now he was in too deep. He was floundering to find a foothold, and if he didn't find one in quick order, he'd drown. There was no future for them. He wasn't the type to settle down with one woman, and she'd made it perfectly clear that this was just a casual hookup for her.

"I don't need my head shrunk," he muttered.

"That's not what I was doing," Claudia said.

"So what difference does it make? We're never going to see each other again after this week. There's no reason for us to confess all of our deepest secrets now, is there?"

"Don't leave," Claudia said as he strode to the door.

"I don't have anything more to say." He opened the door and stepped out into the hall. The lock clicked behind him and he closed his eyes and drew a deep breath.

Though she might be able to control her affections for him, he wasn't quite so lucky. He shrugged into his jacket and headed for the stairs. Until he could put this all into perspective, he'd keep his distance.

He started down the hall and then stopped, the urge to return and apologize halting his escape. Was he using this as an excuse to put some distance between them? Why not tell her the entire story from top to bottom and ask her opinion?

But would she talk to him as a lover, or a therapist? Would she find some fault in the way he handled his father's death or discover some deeply hidden flaw in his character that couldn't be fixed? He wanted to be perfect in her eyes, and the wounds that he'd carefully hidden made him very imperfect.

Hell, he could only guess at how she felt about him. And until he could be sure, Rogan would keep his secrets to himself.

CLAUDIA STOOD OUTSIDE Marshall's room and listened to the chatter of conversation through the door. They sounded as if they were having fun with their movie marathon. She raised her hand to knock, but then paused.

It had been over an hour since Rogan had left her room. She'd expected him to return at some point, but the longer he stayed away, the more she worried that she'd offended him.

She hadn't meant to pry. It was just a professional habit to poke and probe for answers. But then, she'd always worked with patients who'd come to her to solve their problems. Rogan wasn't a patient, and she couldn't force him to reveal his secrets.

And Claudia knew he had a painful secret, something he kept locked inside, something to do with his father. And if she could help him to understand it, then maybe she'd leave him with something beyond the memories of their nights in bed together. They may not have a future together, but she wanted to believe that he'd find love one day.

Drawing up her resolve, she knocked on the door. She didn't like to leave things unsettled. It was her practice to resolve any conflicts with her patients before the end of the session, so that no one went away with hurt feelings. And now, she had to do the same for Rogan.

The door swung open and Leticia, holding a bottle of wine, stood in front of her. "Dr. Mathison! Everyone, it's Dr. Mathison. Please, come in."

"No, that's fine. I was just looking for Mr. Quinn."

"He stopped by earlier," Marshall said, joining Leticia at the door. "He told us we'll be camping again tomorrow night and that we should be prepared to leave at noon for a place called Waitomo."

"Well, then, let's have a group session tomorrow morning after breakfast. Why don't we meet downstairs at ten?"

"We're sorry about the masks," Emma said.

"No apology necessary," Claudia reassured them. "I was a bit grumpy. Under the weather and all. I'm the one who ought to apologize." She smiled. "Well, you have a good night and I'll see you all in the morning."

She pulled the door closed, then headed down the hall to the lobby. Had Rogan gone to his room? It shouldn't be difficult to find him considering the hotel was quite small.

The clerk was tidying a cabinet that held pamphlets for local attractions when she walked into the lobby. "Hello," Claudia said. "I'm looking for Rogan Quinn. Have you seen him?"

"Yes, miss. He walked through about a half hour ago. He asked about a pub. I directed him just down the road. The Thorn and Thistle. Just take a left at the end of the drive and it's a quick walk."

Claudia thanked him, then walked through the front

doors and into the chilly night. She wrapped her arms around herself, the breeze cutting through the fleece jacket she wore. As directed, the pub was only a few doors down. She stepped inside, where loud music mingled with the sound of conversation.

She searched the small crowd for Rogan, then spied him sitting on a stool at the end of the bar. Claudia slipped onto the spot beside him and when the barkeep approached, she ordered a cola.

"What are you doing out?" he asked, reaching for his glass of whiskey.

"I've come to apologize," she said.

"For what?"

"I shouldn't have pushed you. You're not a patient, and I have no right to pry into your personal life. I'm sorry."

He reached out and took her hand, then pressed it to his lips. "I'm the one who should be sorry," he said. "I shouldn't have walked out like that."

"Can we start again?" she asked.

He turned to face her. "You have to give me a break here, Doc. I'm trekking a fresh trail. I'm not used to baring my soul, especially not to someone I'm sleeping with."

"I won't ask you to," she said. "We'll just keep things…simple."

Rogan shook his head. "See, there's the problem."

"Simple is a problem?"

"Part of me wonders whether you could help me sort this out, but I won't really know until I tell you the story.

But if I spill the whole story and I don't like what you have to say, it might ruin everything."

"I'm not going to tell you what to do. That's not the way it works. I just ask questions. And you answer… or you don't. I won't judge you. And you won't have to carry this alone."

"Shouldn't I be lying on a sofa?" he asked.

Claudia smiled. "No. In fact, this is a perfect place to talk—as friends."

"All right," he said. "Ask me whatever you want."

"Why don't you tell me the rest of the story. I have the sense there's more to it."

"My old man was a legend. Everyone knew who he was, and everyone loved him. He was…invincible. He climbed mountains as if he were half goat. And he had a charisma that made his clients think they could accomplish anything. And then, something happened. We've never been sure what it was. Maybe he made a mistake. But he ended up on that mountain. Too high, too late, with no way to get down."

"And he died," she said.

Rogan nodded. "He always carried a small journal with him, and we suspect that he might have written an explanation in it before he died—the truth about why he was still on the mountain. His old business partner wants that journal, probably because there's something that might impugn his character."

"And that's why your brother wants to go get this journal?"

"Yeah. But to me, it's just a stunt. I mean, it's going to make a good story—twenty years later his three sons make the same climb to pay tribute to the great Max Quinn. Only, the great Max Quinn might not be as great as everyone assumes."

He motioned to the bartender and when he had another whiskey in his hand, Rogan swallowed it in two gulps. He winced, then set the glass down. A long silence grew between them and Claudia waited, allowing him time to put his thoughts together.

"There's something else," he finally said. "It's something that could wreck everything that we loved about my father."

"Can you tell me?"

"I've never told another person. Not Mal or Ryan. If it's true it—" Rogan shook his head. "I believe my father was having an affair with another woman. And that they might have had a son together. And now I'm afraid that if we find his journal, there will be something in there, some request for us to…help his other family."

Claudia listened has he recounted the details of the story, stunned by the depth of his dilemma. He seemed to be glad to get it off his chest, the words coming without pause, rushing from him as if he'd kept them bottled up far too long. It was obvious that his fears about romantic commitment were colored by his parents' marriage and his father's affair.

"When did you find out about the other woman?" she asked.

"I think I knew about it when I was a kid. One day when Ryan and I were at the office with him, a woman came to see my father. She'd brought a boy with her, a little younger than us. They argued and she said something about us being brothers." Rogan shook his head. "I didn't remember that, though, until a few years ago when I overheard a couple of climbers talking about my father and this woman—Annalise Montgomery. The pieces sort of fell back together all at once." He drew a deep breath. "So there it is. You can understand why I have my doubts about the Everest expedition." He glanced over at her. "What should I do?"

"I can't say."

"What do you mean?"

"Exactly that. I don't have the answers for you. But I think that when you finally figure it out, you'll know what to do. I understand your need to protect your family. But wouldn't it be better for them to be prepared, so this news doesn't take them by surprise?"

"You're suggesting I tell them?"

"I can't make that decision. You have to."

"You're really not much help at all, are you?"

She gave him a shrug. "As I've said, I'm not a very good therapist." Claudia rested her hand on his thigh. "It's easy to have an idealized memory of your father. You and your family have had years to polish away all the scratches and tarnish from his image until it shines like silver. But he was a real man, with flaws, just as you are. If he's anything like you, he lived his life with great passion. He made mistakes and he wasn't perfect. No one is. So would you rather remember that shiny silver image, or would you prefer to know the real man?"

"I'm not sure."

"You'll have to make a decision," she said. "Before anyone goes up that mountain."

"I'm very aware of that," Rogan replied. He sighed, then slipped his arms around her waist and pulled her close. His lips found hers and Rogan kissed her softly. Pressing his forehead against hers, he smiled. "It's very freeing not to have to carry that around anymore. And now that I've said it all out loud, it's easier to sort out."

"That's how it works," Claudia said. She took his hand. "Come on, let's get back to the hotel. I'm interested in hearing more stories. I'd really like to hear about your ex-girlfriends and why you broke up with them."

"Do you think that's important?" Rogan asked.

Claudia slipped her arm around his waist. "Not at all. I'm just curious."

"And will you tell me about all your old boyfriends?"

"That won't take long. And it might just put you to sleep."

When they got outside, he took her hand, lacing his fingers through hers. "So you don't think less of me?" he asked.

"Of course not. I think it's very admirable of you to keep a secret like that for such a long time. To protect the memory of your father."

"Maybe you're right," Rogan said. "Maybe he doesn't need protecting anymore."

"ALL RIGHT, EVERYONE, why don't we take a moment to talk about the challenges and the successes that we've had on our trip so far. The plane ride over was a bit dodgy, but since then we've made some significant progress. Tell me about your outing yesterday afternoon. How did that go?"

Rogan watched her from a nearby sofa, the morning newspaper spread out in front of him. They'd asked if he wanted to participate, but he'd begged off, choosing to listen from a safe distance away. In truth, since he and Claudia had revealed most of their secrets to each other, he felt a bit uncomfortable around her. Vulnerable. She'd said she didn't think worse of him, but how could he be sure? Maybe she'd already begun to see him as something less than he once was.

Rogan had always prided himself on his ability to conquer any obstacle put in front of him. And he'd been able to do that with mountains and glaciers and jungles and deserts. But he hadn't been able to conquer his childhood.

He knew in his heart that there were still open wounds, wounds that were so deeply hidden even he couldn't find them. But to admit a weakness like that was to give the past more power than it deserved. He was a man, not a boy. And he was strong enough to put the past behind him.

"Why can't we stay here?" Leticia asked. "I really want to go back to Hobbiton."

"I like it here at the hotel," Emma said. "It's nice to have a shower. I used almost all my disinfectant wipes at the campsite, and I need to buy more before we camp again."

"I preferred the first hotel," Marshall said. "I found a dead spider on my windowsill in my room last night. Where there's one, there's a hundred."

Claudia drew a deep breath. "Why don't we talk about the positive things we've experienced? Eddie, why don't you start? I understand you were the tour guide yesterday. How did it feel to be in charge?"

"I hate it here," Eddie said, his gaze darting around the group. "Too many people. It was better when we were camping."

Rogan surveyed the group. They'd all been so focused the night before, and now it seemed they were about to go off the rails again. What was it? Were they trying to prove to Claudia that they still needed her? Or were they uneasy about something else?

She glanced over at him and he shrugged.

"There were too many bugs at that campsite," Marshall said.

"It was outdoors," Millie chimed in. "What do you expect, all the bugs will just leave because you're there? Bugs are supposed to live outside."

"Millie is right, Marshall."

"But my tent was too small," Millie continued. "If we're going to camp again, I want a bigger tent. The people at the next campsite over had a huge tent. I'd prefer one of those."

"All right, let's just stop for a moment," Claudia said, frustration creeping into her voice. "If you don't want to talk about positive experiences, then I have something I want to share."

The group suddenly fell silent and they all turned their attention to her. Rogan put the newspaper down and watched her, wondering how she was planning to get everyone back on track.

"I've often instructed you that in order to make any sort of progress, you have to be honest with yourself. But that's not always enough. I—"

"I knew it!" Emma cried. "Didn't I tell you, Lettie?"

"Tell her what?" Millie asked.

"Romance," Eddie said in a goofy voice.

They all stared at him aghast. Usually, he barely spoke in group, and now he had an opinion? "That is not what I wanted to talk about!" Claudia cried.

"Then it *is* true? You admit it?" Emma said.

"We may be a wee bit self-absorbed, Dr. Mathison, but we're not blind. Maybe you should practice what you preach," Leticia said.

Rogan's initial instinct was to jump in and defend Claudia. After all, he was the other half of the problem they were discussing. But instead, he held back, hoping that she knew what she was doing.

"Should we really be talking about this?" Millie asked, her gaze darting around the group, searching for an explanation. "Remember what happened with the masks?"

"We're just saying that it's time for you to step out of your comfort zone," Emma said. "You can't change your life if you don't take a chance. Isn't that how you convinced us to take this trip? Face your fears."

"This trip is not about me," Claudia insisted. "Now can we get back on—"

"But it could be," Leticia interrupted. "Maybe we should make it about you. Maybe it's time for *you* to talk to *us* about your fears."

Rogan chuckled softly. He was witnessing a full-blown mutiny. They'd all turned the tables on her—and him—and now she'd be forced to explain what was going on between them.

They all stared at her expectantly, waiting for Claudia to speak. She looked over at him, her expression silently begging for rescue. He refolded the paper and stood.

"Rogan," she said in a shaky voice, "why don't you explain what you have planned for us today."

"You're changing the subject," Emma said.

"Yes," Rogan agreed. "You're changing the subject."

"Oh, so now you're going to join the group?" Claudia asked.

"Yes. In fact, there's something I'd like to discuss."

"Yes," Emma said. "Join us."

"All right." He sat down across from Claudia and forced a smile. "I've arranged an interesting activity for us today. It's about a ninety-minute drive, so we should leave right after group. We'll get lunch on the road. And we *are* going to camp tonight." He held up his hand. "No whinging."

"I like camping," Eddie murmured.

"Do you have anything you want to discuss?" Emma asked Rogan. "Something more interesting than today's itinerary?" She cupped her chin in her hand and fixed him with a curious stare.

"Emma, Rogan isn't part of the group," Claudia scolded.

"Yes, he is," Emma countered. "I say we should make him an honorary member for the rest of the trip.

Vote?" Everyone in the group raised their hands on command. "There you go, mate. You're in."

"You can talk about whatever you want in group," Leticia continued. "Complete honesty, that's what we're all about."

He gave Claudia a wary look, and she shrugged. "Well," Rogan began, "I'm very pleased at how the trip is going. I think we've made some progress, but we still have some challenges ahead."

"What are your fears?" Leticia asked.

"I really don't—"

"Honesty," Emma repeated.

Rogan paused then decided to go with it. "Well, I'm afraid one of you might just freak out on me. I'm not sure how I'd handle that, but I—"

"No, no, no," Millie said.

Eddie chimed in next. "Your personal fears. Like, you're afraid of commitment. Or success. Or small rodents."

Rogan couldn't help but chuckle, then realized that wasn't the proper response in a group of phobics. "All right, I do have a thing about snakes. Not a big fan."

"I thought you said there were no snakes in New Zealand," Marshall said.

"No poisonous snakes, no. But I've run into some monsters on some of my trips. And they just give me the collywobbles."

"I'm afraid of heights," Leticia stated. "It's called acrophobia. Acro. Like acrobats, that's how I remember it."

"But you came here in a plane," Rogan said.

"I was completely pissed," Leticia replied. "I drank half a liter of wine before I got on board. I don't remember most of the flight. Have you ever been in love?"

"Lettie!" Claudia gave her a stern look. "That's not an appropriate question."

"I disagree," Emma said. "Who thinks it's an appropriate question? Vote."

They all raised their hands and Rogan realized this was more about curiosity than mental health. But he decided to humor them. "No," Rogan said. "Never been in love."

"Hmm." Marshall nodded. "Why is that?"

"I guess I never met the right girl."

As if on cue, they all swung their attention to Claudia, and her cheeks flushed in embarrassment. "Maybe you could talk about your father," Claudia suggested.

He paused, uncomfortable with the suggestion. But this was what group was about, and it *had* helped to open up about it to her earlier. "My father died when I was a kid. He was on a climb of Everest. They found his body about six months ago and now there's talk about mounting an expedition to recover his effects. They want me and my brothers to go, but I'm not sure I'm ready for that. That's been on my mind a lot."

"Isn't Mount Everest the world's highest mountain?" Leticia asked.

"There are no bugs on Everest," Marshall said.

"Aren't you afraid?" Millie asked. "That you might die, too?"

"No," Rogan said. "I'm an experienced climber and I don't take a lot of risks. I'm not afraid of that."

"What then?"

"I'm afraid that this might change things within our family. There were so many questions about what happened to Dad, and I'm not sure we truly want to know all the answers."

"Why not?" Marshall asked. "I always like to know the answers."

"Perhaps you could talk to us about how you handle your fears. You work in a dangerous profession," Claudia said. "Aren't you ever afraid on the job?"

"Not for myself," Rogan said. "I'm concerned for my clients. There's risk, but it's calculated and I control most of the factors."

"Why do you do it?" Claudia asked.

"I'm more alive when I'm balancing on the edge. There's a rush that you get when you push yourself beyond your physical and psychological limits. It can make you feel invincible. I think you're all experiencing a bit of that yourselves."

"But we're not invincible," Leticia murmured. "No one is. Your father wasn't."

Rogan quickly nodded. "That's true."

"Is that why you've never been in love?" Emma asked.

Claudia groaned softly. "Emma, I really don't—"

But Rogan didn't mind. The rapid-fire questions were all part of the process, and he trusted them. They of all people wouldn't judge him. "Maybe," Rogan said. "Probably. I saw what his death did to my mother and…"

"You internalized it," Eddie said.

"You promised yourself you'd never experience that kind of loss," Leticia cried.

"You have to get over that," Marshall said. "It's important to be open to love. You never know when it's going to find you."

"Yes," Emma said, staring across the circle at Marshall. "You're right, Marshall. You just never know."

"Don't run away from your problems. Face them," Eddie said in a tremulous voice.

Claudia stood up. "Very good, Eddie. Everyone, excellent insights. Why don't we continue this tonight?"

"Well done," Leticia said, patting Rogan on the shoulder. "Do you feel better?"

Rogan pushed to his feet. "Actually, I do." He drew a deep breath. "All right then. I reckon we've solved all my problems. Thank you. I'm just going to grab the bags and load them into the van while you finish up."

"I'll give you a hand," Claudia said. "Group, why don't you finish up without me. Good session."

Claudia called out to him, and Rogan slowed his pace.

"I'm sorry," she said.

"We seem to be saying that to each other a lot lately." He glanced over at her and shook his head. "No worries. I saw that you needed help and I decided to step in."

"I was trying to deflect their attention. They seemed to want to discuss my personal life. More specifically, *our* personal life."

"At least they're not obsessing over their own problems."

"Oh, they'll do just about anything to avoid their own problems."

"Maybe I should develop some phobia to keep them occupied," he teased. "Surely, you must have a spare one I could use for the rest of the week?"

"Seriously, though, it might be good for you to join our group. To talk about how you handle fear." Drawing a deep breath, she forced a smile. "It could help."

He stared at her for a long moment. In truth, he was willing to do anything to make her happy. She meant more to him than any other woman he'd ever known— beyond his mother and his sister.

He'd tried to keep his emotions in check, but with Claudia, it was impossible. He was desperate to get closer to her, and the only way to do that was to open his soul and let her look inside. Even if it meant letting her see the real Rogan Quinn, the man who couldn't commit, the man who was terrified of needing and wanting something more in his life.

Why couldn't he fall in love and live happily ever after? The only thing stopping him was his own irrational fears. And even if Claudia wasn't the one to complete his life, at least she had opened his eyes to the possibilities, and for that, she'd always own a piece of his heart.

"Maybe I should develop a fear of you. Claudophobia," he murmured, pulling her into his embrace. He kissed the top of her head and she snuggled against him.

6

They arrived at Waitomo in the midafternoon, a merry little band of adventurers. To Claudia's relief, the group's worry about the mask incident had disappeared after their earlier session and they were all excited to see what Rogan had planned for them. Once they all got out of the van at the car park, Rogan explained the day's activities.

Waitomo was famous for its underground caves. Visitors could paddle or hike through them, they could drop down into deep tomos on ropes and slide down rushing waterfalls. Rogan suggested a different activity for each of the group members, specifically designed to test their fears.

He asked Emma to throw away her antibacterial wipes, put on one of the communal wetsuits and try the water slides. Both Marshall and Millie were given tickets to the glowworm caves, an activity that combined worms and a claustrophobic environment. And Leticia was instructed to take the chance to abseil down into a cave via a rope and harness. As for Eddie, Rogan instructed him to spend the afternoon riding a boat through the caves and talking to strangers.

Claudia listened as he gave them each a pep talk, telling them that there was nothing that they couldn't conquer if they stood up to their fears. To her surprise, each one seemed more excited than wary of their special assignments, and they hurried off in their different directions the moment Rogan gave them the word.

He stepped to her side and draped his arm around her shoulders. "So, Doc, what are you going to? Now it's time to face your fears."

In truth, her biggest fear was that she wouldn't be able to say goodbye to him. This was their fourth day in New Zealand and they only had three more nights left to sort out exactly what their attraction to each other meant.

She'd been telling herself it was just a temporary infatuation, something to be enjoyed, like a decadent pudding, then forgotten the next day. But everything seemed to make sense when she was with him. As if all the pieces had finally come together and the puzzle that was her life fit perfectly. How could she live without that feeling? Without him?

But though she was supposed to be an expert at reading people's emotions, she was at a loss when it came to Rogan's. In bed, there was no doubt that he wanted her. But he was twenty-eight years old and he'd never been in love. He'd kept his heart well protected and there was every chance that she'd never be able to break down those walls.

What if she realized that she loved him, that she wanted to spend her life with him, and Rogan didn't return the sentiment? Unrequited love was more cruel than never experiencing love at all.

A shiver skittered through her body as she remembered what they'd shared yesterday afternoon, the power of their physical attraction. He had controlled her every reaction, his touch demanding nothing but a shattering response from her body. Claudia had never enjoyed surrendering control, in any part of her life, but with Rogan, she *wanted* to let go.

Perhaps her attempt to get inside his head was her way to grab that control back, before she completely lost the strength to deny him. If she found something lacking in him, some flaw in his character, she might rationalize her way out of love. She could convince herself that no matter how strongly she felt, he wasn't capable of reciprocating her love. She wasn't supposed to judge him, and yet how else could she protect herself?

But the more time they spent together, the more Claudia believed that even if they weren't perfect as individuals, they were at least perfect for each other. Could she get him to believe the same?

She reached out and took his hand, slipping her fingers through his.

"Maybe we could just sit," she suggested. "We don't have to talk."

"I have the perfect thing," he said.

Perfect, she mused. There was that word again. Was he also searching for some flaw in her, hoping she might come up short? Or was Rogan searching for answers in the same way she was? Claudia glanced over at him. He didn't seem to be concerned or overwrought. In fact, he seemed to be perfectly relaxed…content.

Her heart fell. Rogan looked like a man quite happy to live in the present. He didn't appear to be worrying over their future at all. Perhaps the only place this love affair was happening was inside her head. They walked along the pavement, but he refused to tell her what they were going to do until they reached the entrance to the glowworm caves. "This is really amazing," he said. "It's one of the best things to see on the North Island. I'm excited to show it to you."

Worms? He wanted to show her worms? She couldn't think of anything less romantic than a cave full of writhing, smelly worms.

Rogan bought a pair of tickets and a few minutes later they were being helped into a boat. To her surprise, they pushed off before taking on any other passengers. "I rented the whole boat," Rogan explained. "You wanted to be alone. It's just us, the bloke steering the boat and about a million glowworms."

As promised, the cave was indeed something very special, a place she could never have imagined. They drifted along a narrow waterway, through a damp chasm. And yet above, an eerie canopy of tiny lights pulsed, like a million holiday lights in the inky darkness. To her amazement, she realized the lights were coming from the glowworms.

"It's oddly…romantic," she murmured, staring up at the tiny "stars."

Rogan tucked his arm around her shoulders and

pulled her against him, then kissed her. A delicious warmth seeped through her body and she slipped her hands around his neck and surrendered to the desire that pulsed through her. When he finally drew back, she sighed softly.

Claudia heard a sound behind her, then realized the boat man was watching them. "Sorry," she said, glancing over her shoulder.

"No worries," he said. "Happens all the time. You wouldn't believe the number of marriage proposals I've witnessed. We've even had people get married in the caves."

"Oh, that won't be happening with us," she assured him. "We're just—" She paused and looked at Rogan. "We're good friends."

"Right," the boat man said, in a tone that signaled his doubts.

"That's it?" Rogan murmured as he nuzzled her neck. "Just friends?"

"I'm not sure how you feel. I didn't want to speak for you."

"Well, I wouldn't have said *friends*."

"What then?"

"Intimate acquaintances," he suggested.

She smiled. "That's nice. I like it. Intimate, because we are. And acquaintances because we've only known each other for four days."

"And what would we be if we knew each other a bit longer?" Rogan asked. "Perhaps a month or a year?"

"I suppose we'd have to see," she murmured.

A long silence grew between them. Claudia wasn't

sure where the conversation was going. Or whether she wanted to follow it. Sooner or later they'd have to talk about the future. It was inevitable. But she might delay that discussion until right before she got on the plane for Sydney, just to make their farewell a bit easier. Rogan obviously had other ideas.

"So, why don't we talk about it," he said.

"There's really nothing to talk about," she replied.

"But what if there was? What if—for instance—we decided that we might want to get together again? After you've gone home to Sydney."

She swallowed hard, afraid to look at him. "Are you considering that? You'd come and visit me?"

"Or you'd come here and visit me," he suggested.

She wanted to throw her arms around his neck and kiss him, but she checked herself. "Yes," she finally said in a shaky voice. "I suppose that would be an option."

He grinned. "All right. I'm rather fond of options."

Claudia wanted to make plans immediately, to work out the details here and now. She needed to know exactly how it would all happen. They both had careers. His gave him the chance to travel the world, hers was firmly stuck in Sydney. How long might he stay with her? A few days, a week, or two? Or would they have tea as he passed through the airport on his way to some exotic location?

"I have a conference next weekend," she said. "But the weekend after that is good."

"I leave for Nepal a week from Monday. I'll be gone for a month, but I could always fly through Sydney on my way home."

"I've got a vacation coming up right around New Year's."

"I'll be in Belize over New Year's," he said. "But maybe after that?"

She could already see that this was going to be impossible. But wasn't seeing him just occasionally much better that never seeing him at all? A week ago, she hadn't even met him and now she was planning her life around his visits. She'd have to be satisfied with whatever she could get.

He kissed her again. "We'll sort it out. I promise."

It was clear that even in the best of circumstances, they'd probably only see each other two or three times a year. In order to have a real relationship, one of them would have to make a major change in their life. He had his family to think of and she had her patients.

"But if we can't work it out, I'll understand," she said.

"You could always come with me to Belize," he suggested. "In fact, you could help me plan some new expeditions. I could be the adventure guide and you could be the psychological guide."

In her imagination, she could see herself walking away from her practice and starting life all over again, maybe even in New Zealand. But reality was a far different story. She'd worked very hard to build her practice and her professional reputation. Her life was comfortable...and maybe a bit lonely. But she was ready to take the next step in her career. Chucking that all away for a man was a huge risk, and one Claudia wasn't sure she ought to consider.

Then there was her father. She couldn't leave him alone to fend for himself in his old age. Though he didn't need her now, there would come a day when he would be dependent on her help. She couldn't uproot him and expect his life to be jolly. Because of his phobia, he would have to live the rest of his days in his house, comfortable with his surroundings.

So, in truth, she wasn't free to leave. She couldn't dream of a future tramping around the world with Rogan. Her life was on one track, moving in one direction, and if he couldn't hop on board then she'd have to leave him behind.

"YOU'RE GETTING GOOD at that."

Claudia stepped away from the campfire, the teapot clutched in her hand. She set it down next to the fire ring then wiped her hands on her jeans. "I am. I never thought I'd enjoy camping but I'm starting to appreciate it. Food tastes better when it's cooked on a campfire and eaten outside. And it's so quiet at night that I get a deeper sleep."

"I'd like to believe I have something to do with how well you sleep," Rogan said.

They'd spent the previous night together in his tent, Claudia sneaking in after the group had gone to bed and leaving for her own tent in the early-morning light.

"I will give you partial credit for exhausting me, but all this outdoor activity is having an effect, too." She sighed. "I'm going to have to buy a tent for myself when I get home. I could set it up in the back garden and sleep in it every now and then. Build a little fire and cook a meal or two."

They'd made the drive from their campsite at Waitomo to the shores of Lake Arapuni early that morning. Though it wasn't backcountry camping, the site offered beautiful views of the surrounding landscape and lovely walks around the lake from their spot at the landing.

"I thought we'd take a tramp up to the dam this afternoon. There are some amazing overlooks of the water there. And it would be a good challenge for the group if I pushed the pace."

Claudia drew a deep breath and stared out at the glassy surface, while Rogan watched the dappled light play off her beautiful profile. Lake Arapuni was really just a wide spot on the Waikato River caused by the construction of a hydroelectric dam, but it was close to their final day's activities in nearby Wharepapa South, New Zealand's rock-climbing mecca.

Claudia slowly turned around to face him. "This is a beautiful spot, Rogan."

He loved the way she said his name, the sound altered slightly by her Aussie accent. His mind flashed back to the previous night. She'd whispered his name as he brought her to climax, her body writhing against his, her face flushed with desire.

Rogan wondered how long that memory would last. Would it fade over time, or would it be as vivid as it was right now? Perhaps this was why people chose committed relationships, he mused. So that the memories would never fade. But the key was to find someone you never wanted to forget.

Was Claudia that woman? How the hell was he supposed to know? They'd spent four days together and very little of that time alone. And yet, he was absolutely sure that she was different from all the other women in his life. Was that how it went, then? One day he was happily single and the next he was planning the rest of his life with Claudia?

Rogan had never envisioned a traditional life for himself. In truth, he'd never thought much about marriage, at least until Kaylee had brought it up. There were plenty of guides who were happily single, well aware that trying to make a marriage work would be far too complicated because of the amount of travel their jobs required.

And then there was the responsibility of a family. Rogan had been the child of an adventure guide. He'd experienced firsthand the crushing fear when his father would leave for another expedition, the realization that each goodbye might be the last they ever had together. He'd seen it in his mother's eyes, the hurt hidden by a bright smile and cheerful words.

He couldn't be the cause of that distress, especially for Claudia. And he'd been contemplating a change of career anyway. But if he committed to a relationship with her, it wouldn't be the change he'd envisioned. She had a career that required her full-time attention. Claudia couldn't just tramp the world with him on his quest to become the next great adventure photographer. In order to be a psychologist, she had to stay in one place.

So if he wanted her in his life, he'd have to make the hard choice to give up his freedom in order to live in her world. Never once had he considered doing that for a woman. Why now? Why her? And what guarantees would he have that he'd feel the same way two or three months from now? Or that she'd even want to be in a relationship with him once the facade of the dashing adventure guide was stripped away. Love was a risk, more dangerous than any mountain he'd climbed.

Rogan watched Claudia from his spot on the other side of the fire. "I wish you could stay another two or three weeks. There are so many places I'd like to show you. I could take you sailing. Or bungee jumping. We could go down to the south island and climb a mountain."

She gave him a weak smile. It seemed as if every conversation they'd had today ended with some comment on the finite nature of her time in New Zealand. Neither one of them could avoid it. But for Rogan, he didn't want to be reminded that she'd be walking out of his life in a little less than forty-eight hours and they'd found no way to bridge the gap of their careers. Unless…was there some way to connect the two?

He kept trying to come up with a scheme that would keep her with him, even for just a few more days. But then he'd have to come right out and ask her to stay, and that came with all sorts of complications. He'd have to explain why he *wanted* her to stay. And that seemed a riskier revelation than any he'd told her so far.

"I should probably go fill up the water jugs," he murmured. "We're going to need water for our tramp."

"I'll help you," she said.

Rogan glanced around the campsite. The rest of the

group was busy around their own tents. "Marshall, we're going to get water. When everyone is finished, let them know we'll be going on a hike and remind them to wear sturdy shoes."

"Okay, Rogan," he called.

When he reached Claudia's side, Rogan took her hand and pulled her away from the campsite and down a narrow trail. He dropped the jugs and grabbed her around the waist, pulling her into the shadows of a large bush.

"What are you doing?" she asked.

He cupped her face in his hands and kissed her, molding her mouth to his until she surrendered. Her fingers clutched at his jacket, and when he drew back, her lips were damp and her face flushed. "We should have stayed in town," he murmured, pressing his forehead against hers. "Right now, all I really want is you, naked, in a big, comfortable bed."

"No, we only have a few more days. I want the group to have a few more challenges. We'll spend our last night in town."

Rogan groaned. "Our last night. I don't like the sound of that."

"You've really been wonderful," she said. "I couldn't have hoped for a better trip. And after the start we had, I didn't have great hopes that it would be a success. But this adventure is turning out well."

"It's been my pleasure," he said.

"No, it's been *my* pleasure," Claudia teased. "I've realized that I don't take the time to appreciate life. I've been so consumed with my patients' lives that I've forgotten to live my own."

"I can understand. I'm in the same place."

"You don't think you live your life?" she asked.

"Not the way I'd want to. I visit all these astounding locations but I spend every expedition worrying about clients and timetables and budgets. I summited McKinley not too long ago and I stood in that magnificent spot and felt nothing but impatience and irritation because I had to turn around quickly and get my clients safely off the mountain."

"What would you like to do?"

He shrugged. "Get away. Figure out the rest of my life. Problem is, I can't leave Mal and Ryan with all the work. The business supports my mum and my sister, and now Mal wants a family. I have to step up. Perhaps I'll get my chance someday."

"If I were your therapist, I'd encourage you to live your life for yourself."

"And I would tell you I can't. I have responsibilities. Life can't always be perfect."

"Well, you do what you do very well," she said.

"And will you be coming back for more?"

She thought about his question for a moment, then nodded. "Yes. I'd like to. But first I'm going to have to evaluate whether the trip has any lasting effects on the group. If they return to old habits when we get home to Sydney, then I'm not sure what I'll do. My plans to write a book about an innovative new therapy might have to be put on hold if that therapy doesn't actually work."

"I think it's working," he said, grabbing the water jugs.

They started off on the trail and as they walked, Rogan thought about an idea that had been tumbling around in his mind for the past few days. Though it wasn't a scheme to get her to stay, it was at least a way to get Claudia to return to New Zealand. But he hadn't quite worked out all the wrinkles yet. And Rogan had to admit he was afraid she might not have any interest in anything he had to offer.

He'd never been an expert at reading women. He could charm them and lure them into his bed, but beyond their sexual needs, he was usually at a disadvantage. What was going on inside Claudia's mind? he wondered. Was she trying to come up with an excuse to stay, or was she anxious to put their short-lived affair behind her?

Ask her. Ask her. In his mind, he knew it was the right step, but he wasn't prepared to hear that she didn't return his feelings. And though she could be brutally honest, Claudia also had an uncanny way of keeping her own emotions well hidden behind a professional front.

"I suppose you're keen to get home to your normal life," he said.

"I'll have a lot of anxious patients waiting for me there," she said. "Some of them weren't thrilled that I was leaving for a week, but they're all stable enough to get along without me for a couple of days."

"What would happen if you just quit?" he asked.

She gave him a sideways glance. "They wouldn't be happy," she said. "If I decided to leave my practice, I'd have to ease out of it very slowly. I never really worked it out."

"I thought you said—"

"Oh, I've considered quitting and taking a full-time teaching job. But I've never sorted out the mechanics of leaving my practice. Even if I did go into teaching, I'm sure I'd still keep office hours, at least for a while."

So there he had it. All her talk about getting out of private practice was just talk. She didn't want to change her life. He'd known from the start that this was supposed to be all about pleasure, but somehow, he'd convinced himself that he was falling in love with her. And now Rogan would have to talk himself out of it.

"I guess we're both in the same spot," he murmured. "Too many responsibilities to other people, not enough time for ourselves. Maybe we both need therapy."

THE ARGUMENT BEGAN on the hike to the Arapuni Dam. The group had started out in an enthusiastic mood, but as the trail got more difficult and they began to tire, tempers began to flare. But it was when Rogan challenged the group to take a more difficult route and the women overruled his request, that the fracture grew deeper.

Claudia could see an explosion coming, and she thought about asking Rogan to turn around. But he was leading the team at a brisk pace, pointing out interesting sights along the way and barely noticed the snide comments and soft whispers. "Women just don't take as many risks in their lives," Marshall said.

"You can't say that," Emma shouted. "That's entirely sexist. Dr. Claudia, tell him that's sexist."

"Perhaps you can explain what you mean by *risk*, Marshall."

"Men prefer a challenge. Men climb mountains," Marshall said. "They race cars and dive off cliffs and jump out of planes."

"And they scream when they spot a bug," Leticia added.

"That's unfair," Claudia warned her.

"I went into that glowworm cave," he said.

"Worms aren't bugs," Millie murmured.

"That place was loaded with worms," Marshall said.

"Worms aren't bugs," Millie repeated.

Marshall ignored her comment. "Besides, I'm not the one who said it, Rogan did."

Claudia called out to Rogan. "You said that?"

Rogan stopped and turned around. "Yeah. I was explaining that I usually don't have a lot of women on my expeditions. That men are more likely to take risks with their lives than women are."

"Well, that's ridiculous," Emma said. She took the opportunity to sit down on a nearby rock.

"It wasn't meant as an insult," Rogan said. "Just an observation. But I must say that when I do have women on my expeditions, they seem to be much more careful and conservative. That's not a bad quality."

"It's not a quality at all," Claudia said. "And you're wrong. The reason that women don't climb mountains is that they haven't been given the opportunity. They're usually left behind to care for the family while their husbands risk their lives for fun. I'd think you'd realize that, considering your father was a climber."

"Right," Emma said.

"Absolutely," Leticia added.

From there, the conversation devolved into a full-fledged argument over the perceived inequalities between the sexes, the seven of them gathered in a tight group on the trail. To Claudia's surprise, Marshall and Eddie stood their ground quite admirably. Usually, in the group, they'd always deferred to the women, but something had changed.

Claudia glanced over at Rogan. There was the difference, she mused. Rogan's masculine bravado had rubbed off on her two male patients. "Clearly we're not going to solve this disagreement this afternoon," she interrupted.

"Oh, yes, we are," Emma said.

"Maybe we should ask Dr. Claudia," Marshall said. "How many of your phobia patients are men and how many are women?"

"Phobias are irrational fears. For one to climb a mountain, they have to be without fear. I'm not sure the correlation would be valid."

"You don't have to be without fear," Rogan said. "If a climber forgets his fear, he's doomed. He'll surely make a mistake that will get him killed."

Was that what it was like to surrender to love? Claudia wondered. She'd assumed love was the absence of fear, but maybe you couldn't really love unless you had something to fear—loss, heartbreak, betrayal.

"That's why I'm afraid of spiders," Marshall said.

Claudia shook herself out of her thoughts. "What?"

"They can kill you," Marshall continued. "New Zealand has only one native spider that's poisonous. The katipo. The redback and the white-tail spider can be found in New Zealand, but they aren't native."

"Spiders aren't insects," Millie said softly.

Marshall turned to her. "What?"

"You always say you're afraid of insects. But spiders aren't insects. Neither are worms. Insects have six legs and spiders have eight. And worms don't have any legs. And they don't have antennae. Insects have antennae."

"What do you know?" Marshall shot back.

"I know that spiders aren't insects," Millie said. "I've been wanting to tell you that since you joined the group. But...but I was afraid. Until now."

That got everyone started again, and the argument grew so loud that a pair of passing hikers cast irritated looks in their direction. Rogan stood off to the side, waiting patiently as Claudia attempted to resolve the conversation in a positive way. But the moment it seemed as if she could get the group on track again, one of them would go off on a tangent and the rest would follow.

"All right!" Rogan finally shouted. "Enough."

Emma continued on her rant and he gave her a glare that stopped her cold.

"I'm the guide, and as the guide, I have the ultimate authority. We are going to continue on with our tramp and we're going to leave this subject to your group meeting. Right now, I want you to rehydrate, refocus and keep walking up the trail. Marshall, you can lead. I'll bring up the rear."

Rogan strode through the group, then stood next to Claudia. "All right, carry on."

They all got up and assembled themselves into a line, then, one by one, they followed Marshall up the trail.

The walk tired them out, and when they made it back to the campsite, they each trudged to their tents in weary silence.

Rogan caught up to Claudia as she was fiddling with her tent. "So, do you have anything to say on the matter of men being more accepting of risk?"

"Only that you're wrong. But I'm sure we can discuss this later. When we're alone."

"I look forward to it," Rogan said. He held out his arm to open the tent. "After you."

"You seem to have quite the effect on Marshall and Eddie. In less than a week you've made more progress than I have in two years."

"You call that fight progress?"

"They're expressing their feelings. They rarely do that in group. Whether they're right or they're wrong, at least they've found the courage to speak up. And Millie! She never steps into a conflict. Did you hear her? 'Spiders are not insects.' This trip is having a more profound effect on them than I thought. Maybe they should stay with you and I should leave."

"Or maybe you should bring them back for another week," Rogan suggested.

Claudia laughed. "Right. I can't bring them back home unless I actually get them on a plane for Sydney. And at this point, I'm not sure I'm going to be able to do that, so we might be here for good."

"Have you ever wondered what this trip would have been like if you'd brought nonphobic people?" Rogan asked.

"What do you mean? As in people with other psychological problems?"

"Or no psychological problems," he said.

"I'm afraid I don't have any patients like that," she said. "Though if I did, my job would be so much easier."

"Yeah," Rogan said. "I guess it would. What would you do if you couldn't be a therapist anymore?"

"That's an odd question," Claudia replied.

"No, it's not. What if you had to give it all up? Would you join the circus or become a nightclub singer in Paris, France? Would you swim the English channel or learn to make pottery?"

"I know what you'd do," she said. "You'd be a vagabond photographer."

Rogan smiled. "I would. I do take good pictures. It's one of the only real talents I have."

"Oh, you have other talents," she said.

"I wouldn't call those talents," Rogan countered. "More like skills."

"I was talking about your magic touch with my group. The ability to motivate them is a rare talent. It's something I don't possess. Maybe you should go back to school and study psychology."

"I couldn't stand sitting in a classroom all day." He reached into his pocket and took out his camera, then snapped a photo of her.

Claudia covered her eyes. "Don't. I'm a mess."

"You're beautiful," he said, "just the way you are."

Rogan moved around her, shifting his position and the angles of his shot. At first she didn't cooperate, but then he teased her into submission and she finally took her hands from her face and continued her work around the campsite. After a time, she barely noticed him.

"There," he finally said, staring down at the camera screen. "That's just about perfect. This is exactly how I want to remember you."

She held out her hand and he gave her the camera. When she examined the photo, her breath caught in her throat. He'd found a spot where the light and the angle combined to make a beautifully composed photograph. Her hair fell in layers around her face and he'd captured her profile, making her appear far more attractive than she was.

Claudia smiled. "I look lovely."

"You are lovely," he said.

"Now I want a photo of you."

He held the camera out in front of him and took a picture. "How about that?"

"I was hoping for something more than a selfie," she said.

"I can't give you a great picture," he said. "Then you won't have any reason to come back for the real thing."

Claudia laughed. As if she needed a reason. If she knew one thing for certain it was that the moment she stepped on the plane, she'd be anticipating the next time they'd be together. Her breath caught in her throat. Unless they decided to end it completely when they parted.

"I want a better one," she said.

He flipped through the photos on the camera and she

watched over his shoulder until she found one she liked. "There. Send that one to my email account."

"That's not me," he said.

"Sure it is."

Rogan shook his head. "No, that's Ryan. My twin brother."

Claudia gasped. "You have a twin brother? Why didn't you mention that?"

"I think I must have," Rogan said, shrugging. "I've mentioned him before, haven't I?"

"But you didn't say he was your twin."

Rogan studied her expression for a long moment. "I guess we don't know everything about each other."

"I guess not," she said. Claudia turned away from him and headed toward her tent.

"Where are you going?" Rogan called.

"I'm just going to change. I'm a bit chilled and my feet are damp."

She crawled into the tent, then closed the flap. Pulling her sleeping bag up around her, Claudia fought a wave of shivers. This was how it was with them, she mused. Everything was moving along nicely and then something would happen to remind her that she really didn't know Rogan at all.

They'd been together less than a week. Did she really expect that she'd learn every little detail about his life? Yet, if she didn't know him, how could she possibly love him? Maybe this feeling was all just a fantasy, some overblown physiological response that would quickly fade once they were apart.

People didn't fall in love in a matter of days. She'd

never believed in love at first sight, and she wasn't going to start now. So what was she feeling? And would it ever stop?

For once, Claudia wanted answers to her own questions. The problem was, she wasn't sure who could help her get them.

7

"COME ON, EDDIE," Rogan shouted. "Don't look down, just keep moving up."

He stared up the sheer rock wall, realizing that for a novice climber, thirty meters was a long drop. Rogan had free-climbed rock faces three times that height without a second thought, but he'd been climbing trees and buildings and roof ridges since he was a kid. Eddie barely left his apartment most days.

"You're doing great, Eddie," Claudia called. She groaned softly. "Oh, God, just make sure he doesn't freak out."

"He's fine," Rogan said. "Look at him go."

"Are you sure that rope will hold?"

"These climbing instructors are experts," Rogan said. "Joe has guided for us before and I trust him."

"Good. Because I wouldn't want to kill one of my patients."

"Now you understand what I go through every day of an expedition," Rogan said.

"Really? This sick sensation in the pit of your stomach? I feel like I'm going to vomit."

"I think that may be because we didn't get any sleep last night," he said, watching Eddie shinny across the rock face to find another handhold. He slipped and Claudia screamed, then clapped her hand over her mouth. Rogan wrapped his arm around her waist. "You're not helping him. If you don't believe he can do it, then he won't believe it."

They watched in silence as he climbed the final ten meters. When he reached the top, Eddie threw his fist into the air and whooped. A few seconds later, he abseiled back down the cliff, kicking away from the rock until his feet hit the ground at the base of the wall.

The instructor helped him out of the harness, and when Eddie twirled around, Rogan couldn't help but laugh. The guy had the biggest grin on his face, so unusual for him that he was barely recognizable. Rogan strode up to him and pulled him into a fierce hug.

"You rocked it," he said. "Well done, you."

"Thanks," Eddie said. "It was amazing. I was terrified and yet I didn't want to stop." He looked over at Claudia. "This has been the best thing that's ever happened to me."

He hurried over to the rest of the group and they clapped him on the back and offered their own congratulations.

"That just made the entire trip worth it," Claudia said.

"You should try it next," Rogan said.

"No, no, no," Claudia said. "I'll let one of the others go. I don't want to take their turn."

"Come on, Claudia. You have to give it a go. Show them who you are. I'll climb it with you, if you want me to." He stared down into her eyes. "You need to challenge yourself."

She nodded. "You're right. I mean, I have to practice what I preach, right? But what if I freeze up there? What if I get halfway up and I can't go any farther? I don't want to make a fool of myself."

"I'll be with you," he said.

As she approached the wall, the group noticed what was happening and they began to cheer and shout for her. Eddie came up and gave her a few hints as Joe, the instructor, strapped her into the harness. Then Joe called to his partner at the top of the wall and they both grabbed hold of a rope.

"I'll be right below you," Rogan said, handing her a pair of climbing gloves.

She slipped them on. "So if I fall, I'll take you down with me?"

"You're roped in. You won't fall," Rogan assured her. He strapped her helmet on, then slapped it gently. "You're good to go. Take it slowly and don't look down."

Claudia closed her eyes and took a deep breath. "I can do this. I can do this."

She found the first foothold and pulled herself up. Rogan watched as she pressed her body against the rock and held on for dear life. "That's it," Rogan said. "Just keep moving up, one step at a time."

"Where are you?"

Rogan quickly scampered up behind her. "I'm right below you," he said, his voice calm. "You're doing well."

She climbed a bit farther, then stopped as she searched for a handhold. "It's about three inches to the right," Rogan said.

They were nearly halfway up the wall before she paused to look up at the top. Then, as if she'd forgotten his instructions, Claudia glanced down. In that instant, her saw her body stiffen and her grip tighten. Her knees began to shake and Rogan cursed softly.

"You all right?" he asked.

"I—I looked down."

"Yeah, I noticed that. You're still strapped in. You can either go up or go down. What are you going to do?"

"I don't know," she replied.

"Just push away from the rock and they'll lower you down."

When she didn't move, he traversed out from beneath her and free-climbed to a spot right next to her. She stared at him, her eyes wide. "I'm making a fool of myself, aren't I."

"No," Rogan said. He gripped the rock with one hand and reached out to tuck a lock of hair beneath the strap of her helmet.

Claudia risked another glance down, then met his gaze, her eyes frozen with panic. "Where is your rope and harness?"

"I don't need a rope," he said. "This wall is an easy climb for me."

"No," she said. "Go down, go down. No, no, no."

Tears flooded her eyes and she started to gasp for breath. "I'm not going to go up until you go down."

"You sure?" Rogan asked.

Claudia nodded.

"All right." He climbed down the face using the same footholds he'd used on the way up. Fifteen seconds later, he dropped to the ground, then peered up. She was still in the same spot. "Okay, I'm down," Rogan called.

With a shaky hand, she reached out and searched for a handhold. Slowly but surely, Claudia worked her way higher. Rogan smiled as she began to climb with more confidence, and though she struggled a few more times along the way, she finally reached the top.

After a few words with the instructor, Claudia braced her feet on the wall and began to abseil down. Rogan was there to help her out of her harness. But instead of being pleased with herself, her expression was clouded with anger. She refused to speak to him and when she was free of the ropes, she stalked off in the direction of the van. Rogan jogged after her, calling her name.

Claudia's legs were still a bit wobbly and she stumbled, stubbing her toe on a rock. He was there to catch her and Rogan grabbed her arm to steady her, but she yanked out of his grasp.

"Just leave me alone," she said.

"Come on, Claudia, you got up the rock. What's the problem?"

"You!" she said. "You're the problem. You're all about being safe and worrying about your clients, and then you climb that rock without a harness."

"I had a helmet on," Rogan said, smiling.

"Oh, you think that's funny? You could have fallen and killed yourself. People fall off of ladders and die. They tumble down steps and break their necks." Her voice filled with emotion and for a moment, Rogan thought she was going to burst into tears. "And—and it would have been my fault."

He reached out to pull her into his embrace but she evaded his touch, and Rogan let his arms drop to his sides. "If I thought there was any chance I would fall, I would have clipped onto a rope."

"Just leave me alone. I need a few moments to regroup. Please?"

Rogan nodded, completely confused by her reaction. Surely she must understand that he was an experienced climber. The rock face they'd climbed was stable with little chance of any rock shearing off. There'd be nothing to knock him down.

As he walked back to the group, Rogan took off his helmet and ran his fingers through his hair.

He'd noticed the fear in her eyes and he'd only seen that fear once before in his life—in his mother's eyes.

Realization hit him like a brick to the head. Claudia was in love with him. He knew it as surely as he knew his own name. Why else would she have gotten so upset? Faced with losing him to some silly fall, she'd inadvertently revealed her true feelings.

"Jaysus," Rogan muttered. "What the hell am I supposed to do with that?"

He'd never thought that he'd be the one left to sort it all out. Rogan had just assumed his feelings would never be reciprocated. She'd shown absolutely no sign of any long-lasting emotion. Sure, she was sweet and affectionate and passionate in bed. But she'd been very careful not to lead him on. They'd both agreed this was just about physical pleasure and nothing more. What had changed?

"Is she all right?" Emma asked, hurrying up to him.

"What?" Rogan asked, distracted. "Yeah. Sure. She's fine. She just needs a few moments. So who's going next?" He cursed softly at himself for leaving her. "Emma, why don't you go next. I'll be right back."

Muttering, Rogan crossed the distance between himself and Claudia and grabbed her arm. "Come on. We have to talk." He had no idea what he'd done wrong, beyond free-climbing the wall. But he wasn't going to sit around and pretend that he wasn't worried about her—or curious.

Feelings. Bloody hell. All this emotion was starting to get to him. If he wanted to know every little thing that went through Claudia's head then he was going to have to ask her, because right now, he didn't have a clue and she wasn't talking.

"I get that you're angry with me but I don't understand why. You always say that you're honest with your patients, so now I need you to be honest with me. What the hell was that all about back there?"

Tears filled her eyes and Rogan cursed beneath his breath. "Oh, don't cry. Come on, Claudia, I already feel like an arse for making you get on that rock face."

"No, it's nothing you did." She took a ragged breath. "Well, it is something you did. But mostly it's me. I just had a…a bit of a revelation."

"Welcome to the club," he murmured.

"What?"

"What kind of revelation?"

"I—I really don't want to talk about it right now. Just go help the group. We'll talk about it later tonight. I—I'm fine. Really." She forced a smile. "I swear, I'm not angry. Well, maybe a little bit. But if you promise that you won't do anything so stupid again, then I'll be happy."

"I'm sorry," he murmured, reaching out to stroke her cheek. "I don't ever want to hurt you. I need you to know that."

She nodded and smiled weakly. "I do."

Rogan bent close and brushed a kiss across her lips, then pulled her into a fierce hug. "We'll talk later," he whispered. "I promise."

He took one last look into her eyes and saw that the anger was gone. Then he stepped away and walked back to the rock face.

The clock was running down on their relationship, and the last thing he wanted was to spend their remaining time together at odds with each other. They'd sort through this when they got back to their base camp.

THE CAMP WAS alive with excitement during dinner while the group discussed their experiences on the rock wall. Marshall, Emma and Eddie had all made it to the top of the wall. Leticia and Millie both got about halfway to the top before they decided they'd gone far enough.

They had a quick group session and Claudia told them how proud she was of their progress. Tomorrow, they'd spend the day and night in Rogan's hometown of Raglan then head to the airport the following morning. After the flight home to Sydney, their lives would get back to normal and they'd all have to decide what they'd really learned from all they'd experienced on the trip.

As for Rogan, he'd been quietly attentive to everyone, and though they'd managed to act as if nothing had happened, the group seemed rather uneasy regarding Claudia's trip up the wall.

Shortly after dinner, the group decided to walk down to the lake, leaving Claudia and Rogan sitting next to the fire alone. When the others were out of sight, Rogan stood up and held out his hand.

"Where are we going?" she asked.

"I'm going to put you to bed," he said. "You've had a long day."

"And what are you going to do?"

"That's entirely up to you," Rogan replied.

They walked to her tent, and after Rogan unzipped the flap, they crawled inside. Claudia pulled off her shoes and socks, then tugged the sleeping bag on top of her, curling up on her side.

Rogan lay down behind her, dragging her body up against his and resting his chin on her shoulder. For a long time, they didn't speak. Claudia listened to the quiet rhythm of his breathing, her eyes closed, his body warm against hers.

She'd spent most of the afternoon trying to sort out her reaction on the rock wall. In the end, she was forced to admit that it had been pure, unadulterated fear. Not of the height or the climb, but of Rogan falling and kill-ing himself before she had a chance to tell him how she really felt.

When she'd seen him next to her, clinging to the rock with one hand, no harness or rope, she'd panicked. All her doubts about whether her feelings were real had suddenly evaporated. She was in love with Rogan Quinn. Not just attracted to him or infatuated with him. She was undeniably in love. And the thought of him falling off that rock face had terrified her.

But could she say that to him? They'd known each other for a matter of days. And she'd never experienced this dizzying rush of emotion. Though she was trained in analyzing the psyche, Claudia couldn't seem to figure herself out.

"Are we going to talk about it?" Rogan asked.

Claudia rolled over to face him. "I overreacted," she said. "I was just so frightened, for me and for you. I didn't realize that you could climb without a rope. I felt like I was about to fall the entire time I was up there. It was basic transference. I assumed you were experiencing the same thing I was."

It was a big lie, but right now Claudia's emotions were too confusing to explain—especially to the man she thought she loved. She needed some time to consider what this all meant. If she really loved him, then she'd have to find out if her feelings were reciprocated. And if they were, her entire life would change in a heartbeat.

"And you're sure you're all right?" he asked.

"I am."

"Can I kiss you?"

Claudia giggled softly. "I think that's exactly what I need right now."

As his lips met hers, there was no doubt in her mind. Desire welled up inside her and an overwhelming sense of contentment settled into her soul. She *was* in love. It all made sense...except for the part where they'd only met just five days ago.

She'd always taken such a logical approach to life and had advised her patients to do the same. Every decision, every move had been carefully thought out, even with the men she'd dated. She'd never allowed her emotions to carry her away. She'd always believed that to be a character flaw, something that had to be corrected in her patients and avoided in her own life.

But now her heart and her mind were pulling her in opposite directions, and she felt as if she were being torn in two.

"What are we going to do?" she asked.

"First, I'm going to slowly undress you. Very slowly. And I'm going to kiss every spot I uncover, until there isn't a single place on your body that I haven't tasted. Your body is going to be all mine and I'm going to enjoy it for a very long time."

He'd misunderstood the question, but Claudia didn't bother to correct him. Instead, she watched as he slowly pulled down the zipper on her fleece jacket. He slipped his hand inside and cupped her breast.

Claudia's breath caught in her throat and she moaned softly.

"And after I'm done tasting you, I'm going to touch

you. And you're going to touch me. And we're going to stay up all night until we exhaust ourselves."

"Yes," she murmured.

"But first, we're going to get out of these clothes."

His mouth found hers and he furrowed his fingers through her hair as he molded her lips to his. Kissing him had become a powerful addiction, one she couldn't fight. Kissing him was like a conversation without words. His kisses spoke directly to her heart.

He ran his hands along her hip, slowly tugging the fleece pants down until he'd revealed her legs. Rogan pulled them from beneath the sleeping bag and tossed them in the corner of the tent, then slipped out of his own clothes.

When they were both completely naked, he grabbed her waist and pulled her on top of him, stretching her body along the length of his. For a long time, he just held her, their bodies pressed together as if they were designed to fit.

When he kissed her again, Claudia let the last of her worries wash away and focused her mind on the taste of him, on the flood of sensation that raced through her body. This was the man she'd been searching for, the one person who made her feel like a complete woman.

She's always thought there was something missing in her relationships with men, and she'd actually accepted the fact that she wasn't sexy or passionate. There would never be a man to sweep her off her feet, to make her think and behave irrationally simply because she was in love.

But she'd been wrong. All of her fantasies had suddenly become reality. She pressed a kiss to his chest, then slowly worked her way over to his nipple. Her tongue teased it to a hard peak before moving to the other. Rogan groaned and she looked up to find him watching her intently.

Claudia ran her hands down his belly, her nails scraping gently. Her fingertips skimmed over warm flesh and hard muscle and drifted lower, across his belly until she found his hard shaft.

She wrapped her fingers around his erection and gently stroked, caressing him from base to tip. The friction from her touch was enough to cause a groan to slip from his throat and she felt a sense of power. She could make him ache for her, make him desperate to bury himself deep inside of her. She had the power to drive him wild with desire. Or she could seduce him slowly and quietly until they both clung to each other, gasping for breath, caught in the midst of a powerful orgasm.

A frisson of pleasure shot through her as he reached down and touched her, the spot between her legs damp with need. It still amazed her how quickly he was able to bring her to the edge. Usually he was intent on seducing her first, bringing her to her climax before he even thought about himself. But tonight, Claudia wanted to be in charge.

She didn't want to wait, to tease him with foreplay. Instead, she found the box of condoms he'd left in her bag and pulled one package off. She ripped it open and with gentle hands, smoothed the latex over his erection.

Though Rogan must have known what was coming, he gasped as she lowered herself onto him, burying his shaft deep inside her. He held on to her hips, a silent plea for time, as he was already at the fringes of his control.

She leaned close and kissed him, her hair brushing his face, creating a curtain around them. Still, she didn't move, waiting for him to give her permission. Even when he touched her again, she waited, her mind focused on the spot where they were joined and on the delicious sensations coursing through her body.

He felt her orgasm before she did. The moment the first spasm hit, he pulled her up, then drove into her. In one smooth movement, Rogan grabbed her waist and pulled her beneath him, his hands dragging her thighs up along his hips.

She writhed beneath him, shuddering and arching, the orgasm racking her body with incredible pleasure. And a few seconds later, he joined her, collapsing against her as he lost control.

He whispered her name and his pace slowed, his breath warm against her ear, his voice sending shivers through her tingling limbs.

Claudia's body trembled and she begged him to stop, every movement sending a delicious ache to her core. He stared down at her, a smile curling the corners of his mouth. Every nerve in her body vibrated with pleasure and she ran her fingers through his hair, pulling him into another kiss.

From the moment they'd met, this attraction had been undeniable. She'd thought that if she indulged in the desire, it would fade and she would be able to walk away in the end with nothing but a few exciting memories. But now that she'd fallen in love, Claudia realized that,

with every minute they spent together, the passion between them was growing exponentially.

It had grown so big and so powerful that it threatened
to swallow up her entire life. And though it brought her
incredible pleasure, it also frightened her. Claudia didn't
want to make a mistake. She would have to be certain
that what they had was meant to last a lifetime before
she took the next step.

"How are you going to explain this expense to Mal?"

Dana stared at Rogan from across her desk, waiting
for his answer.

"Code it as supplies. Oh, and I need some cash. I
have to buy groceries for dinner tonight. It's their last
night and I wanted to do something nice for them."

"Nice?" she said. "Since when are you nice? And
look at these hotel bills. This was supposed to be survival training. How do in-room movie rentals fit into
that?"

"I had to change up a few things in the itinerary,"
Rogan said. "This wasn't a normal group of clients.
They required more...pampering."

"I can see that," she said, holding up a receipt for
minibar purchases. "These expenses will have to be
charged back to the client. Incidental expenses are not
our responsibility."

"Fine. I promise to go through all of the paperwork
with you after they're gone." He held out his hand.
"Cash."

"What are you going to buy?"

"Prawns. Steak. A couple bottles of wine."

"Wine?"

"Let's just call this a new business expense," he said. "There's a chance we'll be doing much more business with Dr. Mathison in the future."

"How many crazy patients does she have?" Dana asked.

"They're not crazy," Rogan said.

Dana's eyebrow shot up. She reached into her desk and pulled out a small jar. "This is a spider that Marshall gave me. He found it in his room and seems to think that it is proof that the hotel bill should be reduced." She pulled out another jar and then another, lining them up on her desk. "More proof."

"They're not crazy," Rogan repeated.

Dana sighed. "I'm not sure you understand how tight things are here. The business is right on the edge. I can't pay the bills with jars of spiders."

"You can have my tip," he said.

Reluctantly, she pulled a vinyl pouch out of the bottom drawer of her desk and peeled off a few bills from a stack. "Who's doing the cooking?"

"I am," he said. "It's just barbecue. Nothing posh."

"You don't have decent plates and glasses," she said. "I'll bring some things over from my place for you to use."

"I was going to use paper," he said.

Dana shook her head. "You want it to be nice, don't you? You'll also need some flowers and wineglasses." She grabbed the money from his hand. "I'll take care of it. Is it just you and the group?"

"You can come if you like. Ryan is home. I don't expect Mal and Amy will stop by, but we could always invite them."

Dana stood up and grabbed her purse. "You must really like her."

"What? Who?"

"Oh, don't play coy with me, Rogan Quinn. Emma gave me all the details when I delivered their luggage to the inn. She said you and the doctor have been having a…a torrid love affair? I think that's how she put it." Dana grinned. "Don't worry, I won't tell Mal."

"Tell Mal what?"

Rogan spun around to find his older brother standing in the office doorway. "Nothing," he said. "Just that I'm having a barbecue at the cottage tonight. For the Mathison group. They're leaving tomorrow morning. I thought I'd do something—"

"Nice," Dana finished.

Mal blinked in surprise. "Really. Well, that's something new. We've never had clients at the bach. These must be very special clients."

"Very special," Dana said.

Rogan glanced back and forth between them. "Very funny. Aren't you a couple of dags." He pushed out of the chair and walked to the door. "I've got to tidy up the place. Don't forget the wine, Dana."

As Rogan walked to the front door, Mal followed after him. "Hey, now that Ryan is home for a few days, I wanted to get together to talk about the expedition. It looks like our financing is coming through, so we should talk about permits and work on rescheduling our trips for that month."

Rogan bit back a curse. Did they have to talk about this now? He had more important things on his mind. "I'm not going," Rogan said.

"To the meeting?"

"To Everest," Rogan said.

Mal gasped, staring at him in disbelief. "You have to go."

"I don't," Rogan said. In truth, he didn't want any part of it. He was tired of trying to navigate the problems inherent in the trip. After discussing the matter with Claudia, he'd come to the conclusion that it was time he took a stand, whether it caused conflict between his brothers or not. They'd probably go without him, but at least he wouldn't be responsible for uncovering the truth about his father and the American woman.

"Why wouldn't you want to come?" Mal asked.

"I have my reasons. The past is past. Just leave it, Mal."

"It's our father," he said, his face clouding with anger.

"And that's exactly why we ought to protect his memory." He slipped past his brother and walked out onto the wide porch. "I have to go."

His dinner with Claudia and the group was more pressing, and Mal wasn't the sort to let something go without a long argument. Perhaps if Rogan could convince Ryan to take his side, Mal and Amy would finally cancel the plans for an expedition and focus on the biography.

"We're not done discussing this," Mal called as Rogan slipped behind the wheel of the van.

"I'm sure we're not," he replied. He started the van

and pulled out of the car park and onto the road into town.

Raglan was a small town on the west coast of New Zealand, a couple hours south of Auckland. Because of its beautiful beaches and great surf breaks, it drew surfers from all over the world.

The town center was quaint and filled with shops. As he drove toward the inn, he pondered the evening ahead. It would be his and Claudia's last night together and he wanted to make it special for them both.

When he reached the inn, Rogan parked the van out front and jogged inside. He found Claudia and the group gathered in the sitting room, caught up in another group session. Rogan strode over to them and they all turned their attention to him.

"You've all settled in, then?"

They nodded, calling out greetings.

"I hope you haven't made plans for dinner. I'd like to invite you all over to my place for a barbecue. A sort of going-away party. I'll pick you up at five, if that's all right."

"Yes," Claudia said, smiling at him. "But you said it was nearby. We could walk over."

The rest of the group nodded their assent. Rogan reached into his pocket and pulled out a spare envelope, then scribbled down the directions. "Great. I'm looking forward to cooking for you all." He paused. "There aren't any food phobias I should know about, are there?"

Claudia glanced around the group. "I don't think there are."

Rogan leaned closer to her. "Can I talk to you for a quick moment? It won't take long."

"Sure," she said. She got up from the sofa and followed him across the lobby.

Rogan drew her into a small sitting room. Slipping his arms around her waist, he gently pulled her body against his. Then he kissed her softly, exploring her mouth with his tongue, teasing at her lips before stepping away. "I want you to spend the night with me," he said.

"We can come back here after dinner," she said.

"No, I want you in my bed. In my house."

Though she still tried to maintain a professional tone around him, the rest of the group was well aware of what was going on between them. At this point, he was past caring. They had one night left together and he was going to make the most of it.

"All right," she said.

"Good. Oh, and I told my brother Mal that I didn't intend to climb Everest with him. I hadn't planned to say anything, but it just came out. You're going to have to analyze that for me later."

Claudia chuckled, then pushed up on her toes and kissed him again. "Look at you. Who would have ever thought you'd enjoy analysis."

"I enjoy you," he said. "All that psychology prattle doesn't thrill me much." He pressed his forehead against hers. "You thrill me." Rogan drew a deep breath. "I need to be off. I have to clean up the bach and make a few things for dinner. Come around five. And tell everyone to bring their swimming togs. I may throw in a few surf lessons."

They walked to the front door together and Rogan stole one more kiss before he left her. They had just this one night. He wanted to make it something perfect, something she'd remember for a long time.

8

STRINGS OF WHITE lights were draped over the weathered arbor, creating a festive atmosphere for their last night in New Zealand. Claudia stood on the deck, staring out at the water.

The sun had set hours ago, and Rogan had built a fire on the beach. The rest of the group was gathered around, recalling their favorite moments of the trip. She smiled to herself. In the end, it had been a wonderful experience, something that she could look back upon with pride.

In the past few days, they'd made fire and built survival shelters and climbed a huge rock. Earlier in the evening, they'd all donned wetsuits and tried surfing. Though none of them had had much success, Eddie had learned how to use a skim board. Of all her patients, he'd made the biggest strides, casting aside the protective shell he'd created and beginning to see the possibilities for himself.

The remaining members of the group had also made

positive progress. But it remained to be seen whether they would regress once they returned home to their everyday lives. And though Claudia had loved her time with Rogan, she, too, was anxious to get home.

The longer she stayed with Rogan, the more confusing things became. She'd nearly convinced herself that she was in love, even though every instinct warned her that what she was feeling was just wild infatuation. She was a psychologist. She recognized all the signs and could analyze her behavior down to the racing pulse and breathless anticipation.

There was no way she could know her true feelings unless she put some distance between them. Claudia leaned up against the arbor post, wrapping her arms around it. He had such big plans for their last night together, and she was reluctant to spoil them. But she was also afraid that there might be promises made in the heat of the moment—promises that they might not be able to keep.

It would be so easy to map out their entire future together, but Claudia was a realist. Though it might feel as if she was in love, this could all be nothing more than an intense physiological reaction, fed by the proximity of an extremely sexy man.

When they'd begun this, they'd been clear that if they indulged their desire, their relationship would only be about physical pleasure, and she intended to stick to that. She had no regrets. If they truly did love each other, then everything would work out in the end. And if they didn't, the feelings would fade and they'd soon forget about their time together and go on with their lives.

It all sounded so simple when she organized it in her head, but in reality, it would be difficult to walk away from him. No man had ever made her feel the way he did, so beautiful and sexy and wanted. He had changed her. She'd leave New Zealand with the knowledge that she wasn't going to settle for anything less than wild passion and undeniable desire from now on.

She drew a deep breath of the night air and closed her eyes. It was so easy to bring an image of him to her mind, to remember the feel of his hands on her naked body, the taste of his lips and the scent of his hair. It was all crystal clear in her mind now. And yet, she couldn't help but wonder how quickly those memories would fade. Or how hard she'd work to keep them just as they were.

Sighing softly, she pushed away from the post and began to clean up the empty plates and flatware scattered around the dinner table. Grabbing the stack, she headed inside. The dishwasher was full, so she set the plates in the sink, then walked to the bathroom.

Closing the door behind her, Claudia stared at her reflection in the mirror, trying to make an honest assessment of her appearance. After all, she wanted to look good on her last night with Rogan—at least better than any of the photos he'd take of her.

She'd never thought too much about her beauty. She'd always been more about her brain. But she had to wonder exactly what Rogan saw in her. She didn't have perfect features. Her eyes were a rather ordinary shade of green. But she did have a nice smile. She forced that smile, then groaned softly. Never in her wildest dreams had she imagined she'd end up with a guy as sexy and confident as Rogan. He was everything she'd never wanted in a man.

She ran her fingers through her hair and smiled. It would have do. There was no time to change now. She was exactly who she was, and from everything Rogan had told her, he liked her that way. And she was beginning to realize she liked herself that way, too.

When she got back to the kitchen, she found him bending over the open refrigerator, the door wide open. Tiptoeing up behind him, she slipped her arms around his waist and drew a deep breath. "I love the way you smell."

Rogan slowly straightened, then turned around in her arms. Claudia's heart stopped and her breath froze in her chest. The handsome man standing in the kitchen looked exactly like Rogan—only his hair was a bit shorter and his face was covered with a scruffy beard. "You smell good, too," he said.

Claudia quickly stepped back, her face warming in embarrassment. "You must be Ryan," she said. She thrust out her hand. "I—I'm Claudia. Dr. Claudia. Mathison. I—I'm sorry, I thought you were Rogan."

"We get that a lot."

She spun around to find Rogan standing in the doorway, watching them both with a suspicious expression.

"Hi," she said. "I've just met Ryan."

"Step away from the girl," Rogan said, motioning to his twin brother.

"Everyone knows I'm the handsome one," Ryan murmured as he retrieved a beer from the refrigerator. He closed the door, twisted off the top and took a long drink. Then he observed them both silently, his gaze jumping back and forth between them.

"We're having a little party," Claudia explained, breaking the uneasy silence. "It's our last night in New Zealand and Rogan was kind enough to host a barbecue."

Ryan leveled a stare on his twin brother. "Yeah?"

"Yeah," Rogan said. He strode across the kitchen and took Claudia's hand. "My brother isn't the most brilliant conversationalist. Say good-night, Claudia."

"Good night," she said. "It was a pleasure meeting you."

Ryan grinned. "Same here."

Rogan pulled her along to the deck. "I didn't think he'd be coming home so early. He usually wanders in after midnight. Everyone is ready to head back to the inn. You've got an early flight tomorrow. And since Ryan is here, we should probably spend the night in your room."

"I wanted to talk to you about that," Claudia said, pressing her hand to his chest. "I know you had plans for tonight, but it might be best if we don't stay together."

He stared down at her and she couldn't help but wonder what was going on in his head. She didn't want to hurt him, but every instinct told her it was for the best.

"I'm sure you have a reason," he said.

"I do. Would you like to hear it?"

"Yeah, I would."

Claudia slipped her hand into his and leaned up against him. "I don't want to feel as if this is the end," she said. "Then we'd try to sort everything out, make plans, make promises. I don't want to do that. I just want it all to be very simple and quiet. I've had a wonderful time with you and I don't want either of us to say anything that would ruin that."

"Are you afraid I might propose marriage?" Rogan asked, slipping his arms around her waist. He pulled her over to a low wooden chair and dragged her down onto his lap, pulling her tight against his body.

"No. I just think it would be easier for the both of us if we stopped here. At a good spot in our relationship."

He didn't look happy about her choice, but in the end, he shrugged. "So, do I get to kiss you one last time?" he asked.

She took a deep breath and nodded. "But there is one more thing. Tomorrow, when we go to the airport, I don't want you to drive us," Claudia said. "I'd prefer if Dana took us."

Rogan frowned. "Why?"

"Because I'm not going to want to say goodbye. I'm going to convince myself that I should stay and—"

"But that would be great," Rogan said. "I'd love it if you would stay. I've got a couple of days before I leave for Nepal. We can do some traveling or—"

"No," Claudia said. "I have to go home. I have patients, I have a practice. And I don't want to stay. I need to put some distance between us."

"Oh," Rogan said, forcing a smile. "I understand. Fine. Great. Dana can take you."

"You don't understand. All of this has happened so fast and it's been wonderful and exciting. But I think we've been surviving on adrenaline, and it's made our feelings more intense than they might normally be. If I were my own patient, I would recommend that we go back to our lives and take some time to consider what happened here."

"And after we consider it? What then?"

Claudia wrapped her arms around his neck. "If we're still…interested, then we can talk. You can call or we'll video chat. Or we can write letters. But we both have to be sure that we're ready for a relationship before we give it a go."

He reached out and cupped her face in his palm. "This week went by so fast. I assumed I had time."

"Me, too," she murmured. "This can't be over. I might have another group of patients who would—"

"No," he said, shaking his head. "By yourself. Just you and me."

"We started out with such good intentions," Claudia said. "How did we end up here?"

"Come on, Claudia. I knew from the very start that this wasn't going to be just about sex."

"Me, too," Claudia said. "Why did you kiss me? We could have gone on as two professionals. What possessed you?"

"I couldn't help myself," Rogan replied. "It felt like the right thing to do."

"Then kiss me again. Kiss me as if it's the last time."

"It's not going to be the last time, Claudia," he said in a stubborn tone. But in the end, he didn't refuse her request. It was enough for Claudia, this tiny bit of hope that what they'd found was real. They'd proceed slowly, carefully, and maybe they could turn it into something more than just real. It might be something that could last forever.

ROGAN SAT ON his surfboard, staring at the shore, watching as the lights came on in the small cottages near the water. The dawn sky was gray and a stiff breeze blew in from off shore.

He'd been waiting for a wave for a half hour, bobbing around in the cold water, dressed in a wetsuit. He closed his eyes and let the motion of the sea lull him into a peaceful state.

She'd appeared in his dreams last night, as she had so many nights over the past month. And when he awoke, it was almost as if she'd been there, in the instant between sleep and wakefulness. He could still feel the warmth of her body against his, could still smell the scent of her hair.

His mind drifted back to the last time he'd kissed her. It had been right there on the deck, overlooking this very patch of water. He couldn't recall exactly what had been said, but he marked it as the last moment he'd been happy—truly happy. As requested, Dana delivered the group to the airport and Rogan stayed behind.

Now, Rogan knew he'd made a mistake. He should have insisted that they spend that last night together. He should have done everything in his power to convince her to stay. It had been the biggest mistake of his life.

He opened his eyes and saw his brother Ryan paddling out to the break. Rogan groaned softly. Ryan had been tiptoeing around him ever since Rogan had returned from his trip to Nepal.

"You're out early," Ryan said, swinging his board around and drifting up to him. "Waves are pretty decent."

"They're okay," Rogan said. He really wasn't in the mood to talk. But then, Ryan rarely had much to say.

"Come on," he said. "Let's catch this next one."

"Nah, I'm just going to sit for a bit longer."

"Now that you're done moping around the house, you decided to drag your sorrows out here? You're ruining a perfectly good morning with that gloomy face. Jaysus, Rogan, pull yourself together. She's just a girl. There are plenty of fish in that sea."

"I don't want anyone else," Rogan said. "I want her."

"Why? What is it about her that's so special?"

Rogan thought about the question for a long moment, then smiled. "She just…fits. We fit, as if we were made for each other."

"Maybe you should just go get her," Ryan said.

Rogan turned to him. "What?"

"Go get her. Pack a bag, buy a ticket and get the hell out of here."

"You think I should?"

"Yeah. You're not going to be happy until you see her again. How long has it been since you spoke?"

"A few weeks. She doesn't know I'm back from Nepal. I wanted to see how long it took before she called me." Rogan cursed. "I guess I have my answer. She's probably moved on to someone else."

"Then go to Sydney and get her back."

"It's not as simple as that," Rogan said.

"Yes, it is. You get on a plane and in less than four hours, you'll be at her door."

"How can I be sure she'll be there?"

"You could always make a therapy appointment with her," Ryan suggested. "With a different name. Then she'd have to be there."

It was a good idea. And Ryan was right. In a matter of hours, he could have the rest of his life sorted. "All right. I'm going to do it. I can't live in this limbo anymore. Either we're going to have a relationship or we're going to put an end to it."

"There you go."

"Can you drive me to the airport? "

Ryan shrugged, then began to paddle for the shore. "Come on, then. Let's go. The sooner I get your sorry arse on a plane, the better."

It took Rogan exactly fifteen minutes to shower and pack a bag. They jumped in the car, but by the time the sign for the Auckland airport passed overhead, Rogan had changed his mind four or five times. Was this the right thing to do, to force the issue? They'd been apart only a couple of weeks. Maybe Claudia hadn't made any decisions.

Rogan shifted in the passenger seat. He'd been in and out of the airport a couple hundred times in his life but he'd never been this nervous. Though he hadn't figured out exactly what he'd do when they met, he was hoping some kind of romantic movie scenario would come to his mind, where they'd look into each other's eyes and fall into a long, deep kiss—no words required.

"Am I doing the right thing?" he asked.

"I think it's a big risk," Ryan admitted, shaking his head. "But then, I haven't had much success with women, so I'm not the guy to ask."

"Should I call now for the appointment or wait until I get to Sydney?"

"Now. Hell, I don't know why you didn't just stay in Sydney when you came through from Nepal," Ryan said. "I wouldn't have had to drag you to the airport and instead could have spent the morning surfing."

"It's not like we haven't talked. We've had a few emails, but I had a rotten internet connection in Nepal. I tried calling, but couldn't get through. I hope she doesn't assume I've forgotten her."

"Maybe you shouldn't call. The element of surprise might work to your advantage. She'll have to remember you then."

"Jaysus, I have no idea what the hell I'm going to say to her."

"You've got a three-hour plane ride to figure it all out, Rogan."

He sat back in his seat and sighed. "Yeah, I guess so. I just don't want to bugger the whole thing by making a mistake. I figure I have one chance to convince her that I'm the right bloke for her. If she thinks too long or hard, she'll realize she'd be better off with someone else."

"You really believe that?" Ryan asked.

"No," Rogan said. "No, I truly believe that this is the girl for me. She's so clever. I mean, not just book smart. She knows how to talk to people, how to get them to talk about themselves. We…communicate."

Ryan groaned. "Oh, you sound like a damned tosser. Actually, you sound like Mal. What the hell has gotten into the water around here? You've turned into a couple of saps."

"You could be a bit more supportive," Rogan said.

"See, there you go. You're talking like a lovesick idiot. 'Supportive,' 'understanding,' blah, blah, blah, 'I'm sensitive.' Blah, blah, blah, 'let's communicate.' I've never met a woman I'd want to spend more than a week or two with."

"I hadn't, either. But after I met Claudia, everything made sense. At least on my end. Hell, Ry, I was the same as you. I didn't believe in it. I thought Mal was mad, ready to marry Amy after just a few weeks together. But maybe he has it right. When you know, you just don't want to waste a second."

They rode for a long time in silence, Ryan's gaze fixed on the road ahead. Rogan understood that this was hard for him. First Mal and now his twin brother. Of the three of them, Ryan had been the least interested in a long-term relationship. He never lacked for female companionship. There was always a woman hanging on his arm. But never the same woman twice. And his relationships, unlike Rogan's, always seemed to end badly.

"So, what do you think about the Everest expedition?" Ryan asked. "Mal says he has the permits. We'd be going with a British team. He also said you don't want to go."

Rogan shrugged. "I know Mal is keen on it, but I would rather leave it alone. What if we don't like the answers we find? I mean, we've been blaming Dad's climbing partner for what happened. What if we find out it was Dad's fault? That it was his own stupidity that put him at the summit so late in the day."

"You're worried about *her,* aren't you?" Ryan glanced over at him. "Annalise Montgomery."

Rogan gasped. "You've heard about her?"

"Yeah. I figured you did, too. Since Dad's body was discovered, there's been lots of gossip floating around. A few climbers mentioned her on my last trip. How long have you known?"

"A long time," Rogan said. "Do you remember when we met her?"

Ryan shook his head. "I've never met her."

"You have. We were just kids. We were with Dad and she came to the office. She had a little boy with her and he looked just like us."

"She has a kid? You think he's Dad's? Oh, Jaysus, Rogan, I had no idea about that. I don't remember a kid." He thought about the revelation for a moment, then cursed. "And what if Mum finds out?"

"Yeah," Rogan said.

Ryan stared out the windscreen, his eyes fixed on the cars in front of them. And then he sighed. "Maybe we should find out everything we can, no matter how painful. He was a human. He made mistakes. What's wrong with that?"

"Easy to say. But you remember what his death did to Mum. I don't ever want to see her that sad again."

"Maybe, if she finally had the answers, she could move on," Ryan said.

"Move on?"

"Don't you wonder why she never married again? Why she didn't even date? Doesn't that seem odd?"

"No," Rogan said. "I can understand now. For some people there's only one person in the world that they want to be with. I didn't realize that until I met Claudia."

"How do you know for sure that Claudia's that one for you?" Ryan asked.

"She was climbing a rock wall and I free-climbed up to her spot and she freaked out. She got all upset that I might fall and hurt myself, and in that moment, I realized how Mum felt."

As they pulled up to the terminal, Rogan reached into his pocket and pulled out his passport. Once he got on the flight, there was no turning around. He was committed.

"Good luck," Ryan said.

"Thanks," Rogan murmured. He grinned at Ryan. "I have no idea what the hell I'm doing. But I really don't care. Whatever happens, at least I gave it a shot."

"Famous last words," Ryan said.

Rogan hopped out of the car and grabbed his duffel from the backseat. He slapped the top of the car, then watched as Ryan drove off. Reaching into his pocket, he grabbed his mobile and dialed the number for Claudia's office. Her receptionist answered after the second ring.

"Dr. Claudia Mathison's office," the woman said.

"I'd like to make an appointment," Rogan said.

"Are you a new patient?"

"Yes. I was recommended by Eddie? Eddie Findlay? He said she might have some space in her schedule."

"Actually, Dr. Mathison isn't taking new patients at this time. Perhaps I can refer you to another therapist?"

"I really need to see her. Could she fit me in today? Later this afternoon? Two or three would be best. I'm sure my problem could be solved with just one session," Rogan said. He winced.

"I'm afraid her schedule is full."

"But I have to talk to her. It's very important. A matter of life and death. I'm sure you understand."

A long silence spun out over the phone line. "Why don't you come in and I'll see if Dr. Mathison can squeeze you in, probably around three or four this afternoon. I can't guarantee that she'll have time but—"

"That would be perfect," Rogan said.

"What is your name?"

"John. John Jones."

"And a phone number?"

Rogan gave her his mobile number and she recorded it, emphasizing that she wasn't sure that Claudia would see him at all. When he rang off, Rogan smiled to himself. At least he knew she'd be there. That was a start. The rest was up to him.

"Good morning, Dr. Mathison."

Claudia strolled through the front door of her office and smiled at the suite's receptionist. She shared Grace Miller with three other therapists, but as the only woman, she and Grace shared a closer bond. "Good morning, Grace."

"You look lovely this morning," Grace said.

Claudia grinned. "I've been walking on the beach

every morning before work. And then I do a half hour of yoga. I feel much more centered."

Since she'd returned from New Zealand, she'd decided to put some of the things she'd learned to use. She'd found that daily sunshine and a brisk walk went a long way in dealing with any stress she had from work. And the yoga had relieved the tension in her back and shoulders. She felt like a new woman.

"Do I have any messages?" she asked.

"Just two. And you've received an invitation to speak at a women's seminar next month. Plus, Professor Crippen called and would like you to call him as soon as possible."

"Did he say what he wanted?"

Grace shook her head. "Do you think he's going to offer you a full-time teaching position?"

"I don't know," Claudia said as she flipped through her messages. "We've been talking about it, but he was concerned that I haven't published. I told him about the book I want to write and he was enthusiastic, especially since the trip was such a success. But I haven't really been able to put anything on paper."

"Why not?" she asked.

Claudia shrugged. "It's still too…fresh." In truth, she'd thought that distance would put everything in perspective, but it had only made things worse. She was more confused now than she'd been the night she'd left Rogan on the beach. "How's my schedule today?"

"Busy. But your first appointment isn't until ten. You have Jenny Forsberry first up, then Eleanor Winfield and then your OCD group at noon." She paused. "Are you all right? Ever since you got back from New Zealand you've been...different."

Claudia carefully considered her reply. She was different. Her life had been turned upside down by a man she'd known for only a week. When she wasn't distracted with thoughts of Rogan, she managed to get her work done. But it was a daily battle against the fantasies.

When she'd been with Rogan, her life had made sense. She didn't have to make lists and agonize over decisions. She knew exactly what she wanted. But without him, she was adrift, searching for that one thing that could make her happy—and knowing it was him.

"I've just had a lot on my mind," Claudia explained.

She and Rogan had talked that first week she'd been home. But then the communication from Nepal had been limited to the occasional email he'd sent from base camp. He was due back any day and she wasn't sure things would still be the same.

"I noticed that you don't have your phobia group in the schedule for today. Will they be coming to group tomorrow instead?"

Claudia shook her head. "No. We're finished with our work. It's time for them to cope with their problems on their own, or find another therapist. I can't do anything more for them."

Grace frowned. "Really? Wow, I can't believe I won't be seeing them again. They've been with you longer than I have."

Claudia drew a deep breath. "They'll be fine. I'll be fine. I'm just going to go through these messages and then we'll go through the billing." She hurried into her office and closed the door behind her, leaning against it as she gathered herself.

She'd hoped that her usual routine would soothe her nerves and she'd forget about everything but work. But as she stared down at the messages, Claudia realized that she'd been waiting a week for him to call, to reach out and reassure her that he still cared. Surely Dana would have called her if anything had happened in Nepal.

"Of course, he's fine," she murmured to herself. But if he was fine, why hadn't he called?

Claudia had always found comfort in routine, in knowing exactly what to expect from day to day. But that routine had become a weight around her neck, pulling her under. If she were the patient instead of the therapist, she'd urge herself to break free, to make a change, to cast off the past and move confidently into the future.

Yanking the door open, she walked back into the reception room. "I have a question. Do you think I'm a good therapist? You've watched my patients come in and out of here for almost two years now. Does it seem as if they're getting better? I mean, are they making progress? Or have I just been fooling myself?"

Grace opened her mouth and then snapped it shut, clearly confused if the question was real or rhetorical.

"Be honest," Claudia urged. "Please. I want your honest opinion."

"You haven't lost a patient since I've been here. Except for Rose, and that's only because her husband got transferred to Malaysia. Oh, and then Bernie, but he moved to a retirement home that had a psychologist on staff. So, yes, I'd say that you are most definitely a good therapist. Your patients love you. When they leave here, they feel better about themselves. At least for the next week."

"So, I'm the psychological equivalent of a bowl of ice cream or a basket of kittens?"

"Puppies," Grace said. "Yes, a big basketful of puppies."

"I'm too nice. That's why they haven't made any progress. I haven't demanded anything of them. I've just let them continue on. The reason no one has left is because I haven't helped them." Claudia shook her head. "I haven't demanded anything of myself, either. I've been content to just maintain the status quo." She turned and strode back into her office, slamming the door behind her.

With a muttered curse, Claudia sat down at her desk and smoothed her palms over the tidy surface. Then, screaming in frustration, she picked up a stack of patient files and heaved them across the room. Papers flew in all directions, then fluttered to the floor.

She pressed her hand to her chest, feeling her racing heart beneath her palm. Emotions. She'd been trying to suppress them since she got home, but letting them out made her feel alive. Love, anger, frustration, desire. Why bother to deny them anymore?

Grace knocked, then slowly opened the door. "Are you all right?"

"No," Claudia said. "I'm definitely not all right. I think I might be having a breakdown."

"Really? Do you want me to call a doctor? I mean, a medical doctor?"

"Actually, it's more a meltdown, not a breakdown. It's just…I try to enjoy coming to work, but it's as if—as if I don't belong here anymore."

"Where do you belong?"

"Where I've always belonged. I just hadn't realized it yet."

"Hmm. Well, I'm just going to leave you alone to deal with this. If you need me, just call."

As Grace closed the door behind her, Claudia put her head down on her desk. Since her plane had left Auckland, she'd tried not to think about Rogan, but what was the point? If it weren't for him, she wouldn't be in this mess. She never would have known that she wanted a man in her life and that she wanted that man to be exactly like Rogan.

She never would have admitted that she wasn't satisfied with her job or that she deserved more from life than she was getting. Like excitement and passion and joy—all the things she experienced when she was with Rogan Quinn.

He'd ruined her—for her life, for any other man who might wander her way, for her general happiness. Claudia had promised herself that she wouldn't fall in love with him and she'd done exactly that.

Her intercom buzzed and she picked up the phone. "Give me a few more minutes, Grace."

"Dr. Mathison, you have patients who are asking to see you."

"But you said I didn't have an appointment until ten."

"These people don't have an appointment. Wait! Hey, don't go in there until—"

Her office door swung open and her five phobics strode in and sat down in their usual places. "We've decided we deserve one last session," Emma said. "And we're going to have one right now, whether you like it or not."

"I'm not going to change my mind," Claudia said.

"Oh, we don't want you to change your mind," Millie said. "At least, not about us." She took a quick breath, then forced a smile. "We think you should change your mind about him."

"Marshall?" she asked.

"No! *Him*. Rogan. If you don't have us, then you should have Rogan instead. He's in love with you and you're in love with him, so go back to New Zealand and tell him how you really feel."

"What if I'm not sure of how I really feel?" Claudia said.

Emma stood up. "Oh, bloody hell, you're always nattering on and on about us being honest with ourselves. Practice what you preach. Be honest. You miss him already. You think about him all the time. You wonder if you'll ever feel the same about another man."

"It's more complicated than that," Claudia said.

"No, it isn't. Watch." She turned and faced the group. "Marshall, I'm in love with you. I never thought I'd fall in love, but I have. I don't know what I'm going to do with myself if you don't love me, but I'm willing to take the chance. And just so you're aware, I hate bugs, too, and if you love me, I'll do everything in my power to keep your life bug-free."

Marshall glanced around the group, then slowly got to his feet. "Is this real?"

"I wouldn't joke about something like this," Emma said softly. Tears swam in her eyes and Claudia reached out and took her hand, giving it a squeeze.

"I—I love you, too," Marshall said. "I've always loved you. From the moment you gave me that little bottle of hand sanitizer, I realized we'd make a brilliant pair."

"You do? You really love me?"

They met in the middle of the room, falling into a clumsy kiss. The rest of the group gathered around them, clapping and offering their best wishes. But Claudia held back, watching her patients, awash in her own emotions.

If it could be so simple for them, why was it so difficult for her? She'd helped them navigate their lives, and yet she was the one who was lost now. "I'm so happy for you," she said, joining in the group hug.

"And what about you?" Emma asked. "Don't you deserve some happiness?"

Claudia drew a ragged breath. "Yes," she said. "Yes, I believe I do."

"Then go back to New Zealand and tell Rogan that you love him," Leticia said.

"I agree," Eddie said. "Take a risk."

"Yes, take a risk," Millie said, her gaze fixed on Eddie. The young man gave her a quick smile and Claudia watched a blush rise in her cheeks.

"All right," she said. "I will."

"Promise?" Leticia asked.

"Yes. In fact, I'll have Grace get me a ticket right now." They all gathered around her in another group hug and Claudia laughed.

"You'll have to tell us about it in group," Emma said. "We want to hear all the details."

Claudia frowned. "We're not having group sessions anymore."

"Oh, we've decided to carry on by ourselves. We're meeting for breakfast every Tuesday morning at the restaurant across the street. They're reserving a corner booth for us. You're welcome to join us."

"Maybe I'll do that," Claudia said.

The group said their goodbyes and then hurried out of the office, occupied with plans for a celebratory lunch. When the door closed behind them, Grace looked over at Claudia. "What was that all about?"

"Love," Claudia said. "Grace, I need you to book me a ticket to Auckland. And a rental car. I want to leave as soon as possible."

"You're going back? But why?"

"I have some things to say to someone and I can't do it over the phone. He's due home from Nepal any day now, and I'm going to be there when he returns." Claudia felt the excitement rise inside her. She had no idea how this would work out, and for the first time in her life, she was jumping in without a plan.

Though she could spend the entire morning running over the pros and cons of what she was about to do and convince herself that it would never work, no amount of analysis would give her the answer she was looking for. Only Rogan could do that.

By 3:00 P.M., GRACE had booked a ticket to Auckland, gone to Claudia's place and packed an overnight bag, then returned to help Claudia reschedule her patients for the next week.

"You have one more appointment," Grace said through the intercom as she sat her desk. "He's due here at three."

"He's fifteen minutes late. Did you call me a cab?"

"Yes," Grace said. "It will be here at three forty-five. That's plenty of time to make your seven o'clock flight."

"This is not the day to start with a new patient. We'll just get to introduce ourselves and I'll have to leave. Maybe we should just tell him to book another appointment, I—"

"He's here," Grace murmured.

"Well, have him fill in the info sheet and then send him in."

Claudia straightened out her desk and waited patiently. A few seconds later, Grace slipped inside the office and closed the door behind her. "This is going to sound really awful, but your new patient is hot! I mean, really, really handsome," Grace whispered.

"Do not start pashing on the patients, Grace. No touching."

"And he's very pleasant and charming. And apologetic for being late. Do you want me to bring him in?"

"That's usually how we do things around here,

Grace. I'll introduce myself, we'll chat and then we'll make another appointment for after I return."

"But you don't know when that will be," Grace said.

"Well, if things don't go well, it could be as early as tomorrow," she murmured.

"Should I send him in now?"

"Just give me a few moments." Claudia sat down at her desk and buried her face in her hands. Maybe going to New Zealand wasn't the best idea. She pulled out a notepad and began a list of pros and cons then ripped the sheet off and tossed it across the room.

"Hey, Doc."

She groaned. Her head had been filled with images of him all day, and now she was hearing his voice. "Hello," she murmured. Sighing softly, Claudia sat up—and froze.

Rogan was standing at the door, watching her with a devilish smile on his face. "That Grace is tough to get by. She ought to play goalie for a pro footie team."

"Oh, my God, what are you doing here? I thought you were still in Nepal."

"I didn't want to wait for you to come to me," he said. "So, I decided to take a chance. I'm in need of some serious analysis, Doc."

Claudia held up her ticket. "I was coming to see you. I have a flight out this evening."

"Great minds think alike," he said with a crooked smile.

"And what are you thinking about right now?" Claudia asked.

"I'm thinking about pulling you into my arms and kissing you," he said.

"Me, too," she murmured.

In a few short steps, they closed the distance between them and fell into each other's arms. His mouth was soft yet demanding, and he kissed her until she was breathless. But it wasn't enough.

Claudia threw all the files off her desk, then pulled him down onto the fine mahogany finish. She clung tightly to the lapels of his jacket and he stepped between her legs and pulled her hips against his.

"I missed this," he said.

"Oh, me, too. Please tell me you're going to stay for a while."

"A week," he said. "Then I have another trip. But I can just as easily leave from here."

"Yes," she said, smiling. "Yes."

He kissed her again, this time taking care to seduce her slowly and thoroughly. At the end of it all, their clothes were disheveled and their hair mussed.

"Can we really do this?" she asked.

"Kissing? Yeah, I'd say we're pretty damn good at it. We're experts when it comes to snogging."

"I meant a relationship. Can we make it work?"

"We can," Rogan said. "From now on, I'll come and go from Sydney, so we'll see each other every minute that I'm not working. And, I also have a plan."

"A plan?"

He nodded, then pushed up and crossed her office to retrieve his bag. Rogan opened it and took out a stack of paperback books. "Look at these. These are all self-help books, books that tell people how to fix their problems—it's a bazillion-dollar industry. But we should be doing that," Rogan said. "We can run trips, challenge trips. They can be about improving a person's physical and mental and spiritual well-being. You could be in charge of the psychology stuff and I'd be the adventure guy. We'd work together."

She sat up and brushed her hair out of her eyes. "That's a brilliant idea, Rogan. Have you talked to your brothers about it?"

"No. But as long as I'm contributing my share to the business, they're fine letting me do what I want. I'll do whatever it takes to make it work. Because I love you, Claudia. I didn't believe it was possible, but you changed me. So what do you say, Doc? Say yes."

"To the plan?" Claudia asked.

"To spending the rest of your life with me."

She smiled. "You've changed me, too, Rogan. And I don't have to think about it. Yes, I love you. And yes to the rest of our lives."

Claudia threw her arms around his neck and hugged him hard. "I can't believe this is happening. You're here...to stay."

He picked her up off her feet and kissed her, long and hard. "Yes," he murmured. "I'm here. And I'm not going anywhere."

Epilogue

AILEEN QUINN SAT at on the iron bench in her garden. She closed her eyes and drew a deep breath of the fresh morning air. All around her, the songs of birds filled the air.

It was a perfect Irish morning, the dew still damp on the flowers, the air clear and the sky blue. Life seemed to pulse all around her. On days like this, she didn't feel like a woman in her nineties. She was young again, full of hope and promise.

The years had passed so quickly, and now, the thing she'd longed for most in her life had finally come to pass. The orphan had found a family. Slowly, the brothers she'd lost as a child had come back to her—in their descendants.

Would this finally be the end of her search? Ian Stephens, the man to whom she'd entrusted the task of finding her relatives, had rung her to say that he'd finally located Conal's lost family. Her brother had left Ireland after World War II for parts unknown. But with diligent research, Ian had traced him to Australia.

"Aileen?"

She glanced up to see Ian walking toward her. Smiling, she held out her hand to him and he grasped it. "I'm so glad you've come. It's been far too long. How is Claire? Why didn't you bring her with you?"

"She's quite well," he said. "But she's teaching today. They called her in for a sick colleague and she couldn't resist going back."

"Well, you'll have to bring her for lunch very soon. I'd like to catch up with my great-niece."

"How have you been? You look wonderful."

"I feel well. Hopeful. Have you brought me good news?"

Ian shrugged. "Some good, some bad." He took a folder from his briefcase. "After Conal left Ireland, he turned up in Australia. He worked in Sydney and late in life, met a younger woman and married her. They had a son, born in 1958, named Maxwell Quinn. A year after he was born, Conal died of a heart attack, leaving his young wife to raise her little boy."

"He was born in 1958? Where is he? Have you contacted him?"

"This is the bad news," Ian said. "He died, quite tragically, in 1994."

He handed her a sheaf of papers, photocopies of newspaper articles from April of that year. Aileen placed them in her lap. "Tell me what happened."

"Maxwell Quinn was quite a famous climber. He was guiding an expedition on Mount Everest and died when he was trapped overnight near the summit. He left behind four children—three sons and a daughter.

All are currently living in New Zealand and working in the family's expedition-guiding business."

"Four?"

"Malcolm is the eldest. He's thirty. His brothers, twins Rogan and Ryan, are twenty-eight and their sister, Dana, is twenty-four. They live in a small town about a couple hours south of Auckland."

"They're the last ones," Aileen said. "The search is over."

"I believe it is," Ian said.

She drew a deep breath and slowly released it. "Good. It's a relief to know that I've lived long enough to find them all."

"And to meet them all," he said.

"Have you contacted them? Did you tell them about me?"

"Not yet. We're still trying to firm up the connections before we go in and ask for a DNA test."

"I'm getting older by the minute," Aileen teased. "I might not have much time. And I want to meet them all, before I shuffle off this mortal coil."

"I'm afraid I recommend caution," Ian said. "We've been very careful to confirm the connection to you before we contact anyone. I don't think it's wise to announce to a family that they're about to inherit millions, only to announce a few weeks later that they won't."

"Of course, you're right," Aileen said. "It wouldn't be fair. Do you have photographs I might look at?"

"Better yet," Ian said. "They have a website. And a blog. The three boys have lived an adventurous life.

Their sister, Dana, has also guided some treks in Nepal and India."

Ian stood and held out his hand. "Come on, let's go inside and I'll show you."

Aileen shook her head. "You go. I'd like to sit here for a bit longer. The sun is so warm and it's such a beautiful day.

"All right," Ian said. "I'll have Sally make us a cup of tea."

"Good."

She listened to his footsteps fade as he crossed the gravel walk to the terrace. "It won't be long," Aileen murmured to herself. "I've put my family back together. There's nothing left for me to do. I'll see you all very soon."

She reached out for her cane but when she tried to stand, she suddenly felt weak and unbalanced. This would not be a bad place to end her story, Aileen thought to herself. It was peaceful and perfect, one of her favorite spots on all the earth.

Aileen waited, ready, consigned to the fact that when it was her time, it was her time. But after a few minutes, she opened her eyes. "Not yet? I suppose there must be some reason You want to keep me here."

She pushed to her feet and started toward the house. A cup of tea would be nice. And she hadn't met these new members of the Quinn family. Once they'd come to visit, she could think about the last chapter.

* * * * *

#811 A SEAL'S FANTASY
Unrated!
by Tawny Weber
Navy SEAL Dominic Castillo has a reputation for always
getting the girl—but he meets his match when forced to protect
Lara Banks, the tempting, unrepentant sister of his rival.

#812 BEHIND CLOSED DOORS
Made in Montana
by Debbi Rawlins
Sexy rancher Nathan Landers steers clear of Blackfoot Falls
and the small-town rumor mill, but beautiful newcomer Bethany
Wilson is offering a naughty no-strings deal he can't refuse!

#813 CABIN FEVER
The Wrong Bed
by Jillian Burns
On a cruise, fashion blogger Carly Pendleton tries to fight her
attraction to "Average Joe" contest winner Joe Tedesco, who
sizzles with raw masculinity. They don't seem to have much in
common...but can she fight the fire blazing between them?

#814 STRIPPED DOWN
Pleasure Before Business
by Kelli Ireland
One impulsive night with gorgeous dancer Dalton Chase leaves
engineer Cassidy Jameson aching for more. But inviting him
into her bed is one thing...inviting him into her life, quite another.

REQUEST YOUR FREE BOOKS!
2 FREE NOVELS PLUS 2 FREE GIFTS!

H HARLEQUIN®

Blaze®

red-hot reads!

HB13R2

Entering her building, Lara felt the weight of the day on her shoulders. She still had hours of homework and eight shows to dance over the weekend. If she nailed this assignment, she'd have the top grade in the class, which meant an internship with a top-flight security firm.

Six more weeks to go. With a sigh, she rounded the hallway to her corridor.

Lara Lee, Cyber Detective.

She grinned, then blinked. Frowning, she noted the hall lighting was out. She'd just put her key in the lock when she felt him.

It wasn't his body heat that tipped her off.

Nope, it was the lust swirling through her system, making her knees weak and her nipples ache.

Taking a deep breath, she turned. "Do you always lurk in the shadows?"

"Hall light is out. Shadows are all you've got here."

"What do you want?"

"I told you. I need to talk to you about your brother."

"And I told you. I don't have a brother."

Not anymore.

"Lieutenant Phillip Banks. Navy SEAL. Ring any bells?"
His words were easy, the look in his eyes as mellow as the half
smile on his full lips.

"My last name is Lee." Then, before she could stop herself,
she asked, "Why are you running errands for this guy, anyway?"

His dark eyes flashed. "Sweetheart, do I look like anyone's
errand boy?" he said.

Lara couldn't resist.

She let her eyes wander down the long, hard length of his
body. Broad shoulders and a drool-worthy chest tapered into
flat abs, narrow hips and strong thighs.

She wet her lips and met his eyes again.

He looked hot.

As if he'd like to strip her down and play show-and-tell.

Tempting, since she'd bet that'd would be worth seeing.

"Sorry," she said. "I'm not the woman you're looking for."

Damn.

Not for the first time in his life, Dominic Castillo cursed
Banks. The guy was a pain. Figured that long, lean and sexy
was just as bad.

He wanted to grab her, haul her off to the nearest horizontal
surface.

Insane.

He was on a mission. *She* was his duty.

He'd never lusted after a mission before.

**Pick up A SEAL'S FANTASY by Tawny Weber,
available in September 2014 wherever you buy
Harlequin® Blaze® books.**

HBEXP79815

No Strings Attached!

Sexy rancher Nathan Landers steers clear of
Blackfoot Falls and the small-town rumor mill, but
beautiful newcomer Bethany Wilson is offering a
naughty no-strings deal he can't refuse!

Don't miss the latest chapter of the
Made in Montana miniseries

Behind Closed Doors
From reader-favorite author

Debbi Rawlins

Available September 2014 wherever you buy
Harlequin Blaze books.

HARLEQUIN®

Blaze

Red-Hot Reads
www.Harlequin.com

HB79816

Can They Take the Heat?

On a cruise, fashion blogger Carly Pendleton tries to fight her attraction to "Average Joe" contest winner Joe Tedesco, who sizzles with raw masculinity. They don't seem to have much in common...but can she fight the fire blazing between them?

From the reader-favorite **The Wrong Bed** miniseries

Cabin Fever
by *Jillian Burns*

Available September 2014 wherever you buy Harlequin Blaze books.